The Sheikh's Forbidden Bride

Sands of Passion, Volume 3

Amara Holt

Published by Amara Holt, 2024.

Copyright © 2024 by Amara Holt

All rights reserved. No part of this book may be reproduced, distributed, or transmitted in any form or by any means, including photocopying, recording, or other electronic or mechanical methods, without the prior written permission of the author, except in the case of brief quotations in book reviews.

This is a work of fiction. Names, characters, places, and incidents are the product of the author's imagination or are used fictitiously. Any resemblance to actual events, organizations, locales, or persons, living or dead is coincidental and is not intended by the authors.

PROLOGUE

Elahe

SIX YEARS EARLIER...

"Ihab, we might get caught," I whisper, my voice muffled by his kisses.

He doesn't stop, and I'm lost in the moment, his hands trailing down my back. If my brother finds us here, it will be the end of me.

"Ihab..." I call his name again.

"Do you want me to stop?" He holds my face with both hands, halting the kiss.

"This is wrong," I glance around, noticing the room we are in is empty.

"You said you'd give me proof of your love. Isn't this the biggest proof? Didn't you say you loved me, Elahe?"

I remain silent, focusing on his beautiful honey-colored eyes, getting lost in them.

"Give yourself to me..." he whispers, bringing our lips back together.

The kiss was slow, like that sweet, slow melody I love to feel.

Ihab lifts my tunic, laying me down on the cold floor of the women's private room, committing the greatest sin I could subject myself to.

I felt his member pressing against my entrance.

In the dead of night, in the silence of the early hours.

Without warning, without removing his clothes, without removing mine, that act tore me apart.

I bit my lip at the relentless pain I felt.

"Please... stop..." I begged, not understanding why it hurt so much, how could people think this act was pleasurable?

Tears filled my eyes, burning my face as they streamed down.

"We're almost there..." he groaned, going deeper, thrusting with force.

I gripped his shoulder, no longer recognizing the man I thought I loved.

I began to feel filthy! What had I just done?

I dug my nails hard into his shoulder, causing him to pull away, giving me the chance to escape.

I turned my body, crawling until I could stand. I looked at Ihab, who stared back at me, terrified.

"What happened, why are you doing this?" he asked, walking toward me.

"Stay there..." I raised my hand, but it wasn't enough for him, and he kept walking toward me "STOP!"

I screamed so loudly, out of fear, fear of what I had just done.

"Are you crazy? They'll hear us," Ihab scolded me, "Or better yet, scream, so your brother will be forced to accept our marriage."

He smiled smugly.

"So that was it? I was just another conquest for you?" I asked with disgust.

"Isn't this what we wanted? Marriage?" He started walking toward me again.

"No, not like this," I whispered.

My eyes flew to the door, which burst open with a crash, and my brother entered, his eyes filled with horror.

"What the fuck is going on here?" Hassan looked at me, his eyes wide as he saw my state, my *hijab* thrown on the floor, completely exposed to another man.

"Looks like the one we wanted has arrived," Ihab declared smugly.

"I'm sorry, brother..." A sob escaped my throat.

"No, Elahe, tell me you didn't do this..." His voice trailed off, the disappointment clear in his tone.

"What's going on here?" My mother's voice broke through the tension.

Zenda acted quickly when she saw our state and closed the door to the room.

"Looks like we're going to be brothers-in-law after all," Ihab chimed in again.

Hassan clenched his fists, as if trying to control himself. It wasn't supposed to be like this. What was I thinking? My brother had just taken over the government of Budai, we had just lost our father. How could I bring such disgrace to Hassan?

At what point did I lose myself?

How? How? How?

"By *Allah*, Elahe, my daughter?" Zenda looks around, horrified.

"Sister?" Hassan calls for my attention.

I look at him, finding in Hassan my safe harbor, knowing that above being the governor of Budai, he is my brother, the one who always listened to me.

I close my eyes, letting another sob escape my throat.

"So, when is our wedding?" Ihab boasts.

"Shut the fuck up!" Hassan walks toward him. "Elahe is just a child who only turned eighteen! How dare you take advantage of her vulnerability, you bastard!"

My brother gets in his face, almost spitting on Ihab.

"Your sister is a fool, she was so easy to deceive," Ihab smiles in Hassan's face.

The moment was broken by Abdul, my other older brother, who rushed over to Hassan, stopping him from doing something worse.

"Brother," Abdul holds onto Hassan's shoulder.

"I'm going to destroy this scumbag!" Hassan tries to ignore Abdul, but it's in vain.

"Stop, please stop!" I plead, not wanting to tarnish my family's reputation further.

Everyone looks at me. My eyes lock onto Ihab, on his sweet words, on how he deceived me, all to take my virginity and force his way into our family, even if it meant playing dirty, trying to force himself on me.

Force? How foolish I am, I gave myself to him willingly.

How could I have thought I loved Ihab?

Stupid, stupid, stupid!!!

Hassan steps away from Ihab, walking toward me, taking my hand. Without warning, he pulls me into his chest.

His hand rests on my back, pressing my body to his chest. I let the tears flow from my eyes, as if a hole had opened up beneath me.

And all my dreams?

How did I let a man take control of my life?

Me, who always dreamed of independence, and the university I so badly wanted to attend?

"*Shhhh...*" Hassan whispers in my ear. "If you don't want this marriage, you won't have it. I am the ruler of this emirate, and this bastard will never control you, my sister."

I raise my head, meeting my brother's intense, pained eyes.

"You'd do that?" I asked.

"I'd do anything to see you happy..."

"What are you saying, Hassan?" I hear my mother ask.

"This marriage is out of the question," Hassan positions himself in front of me.

"What do you mean? Don't you understand? I took your sister's purity," Ihab states the obvious.

"And that's why you will be banished from my emirate. If you speak to anyone about this, I will destroy you slowly. You don't know me. No one messes with my family and walks away unscathed!"

Abdul stands beside Hassan, as if they were creating a barrier to protect me.

My mother said nothing. Zenda never liked Ihab, always warning me that he was a social climber, but I always thought it was just one of the many ways she tried to arrange a noble suitor for me, something Ihab was not.

How could I have been so foolish to give my heart to this man?

No man will ever touch my heart again.

I will become like a rock, one that no one can touch.

CHAPTER ONE

Elahe

"Mali?" I called for my sister-in-law, looking around the room.
"It looks like this will be your new home," Malika sighed, coming towards me.

"Do I still have a chance to escape?" I murmured with a forced smile on my lips.

"Know that I will be your accomplice, and no one needs to know," Malika said, holding my hand with a comforting smile.

"Thank you..." I whispered so softly that the word came out as a breath.

A long sigh escaped my mouth; it seems that what I feared most is going to happen: my marriage.

All because my mother overheard a conversation of Sheikh Khalil, blackmailing him into marrying me.

I know nothing about him, except that he had an affair with my sister-in-law, Malika. She and Khalil almost got engaged, that is, if my brother hadn't forced a marriage with her. A fact that had remained hidden from everyone until my mother overheard Khalil on a phone call, revealing to someone that he and Malika had an occasional affair. Zenda blackmailing him, saying that if he didn't marry me, she would put Malika's name in all the gossip tabloids.

Of course, Khalil would protect my sister-in-law, even though he no longer felt anything for her, he did it out of respect. Accepting the union with me.

And here I am, being the bargaining chip, a union through blackmail. I will marry a man who doesn't love me, a man who once loved my sister-in-law, a man I don't even desire.

Who am I trying to fool?

Since the day Ihab ruined me, no other man has attracted me, or even caught my attention.

I raised my eyes seeing the door of the room open; Zenda walked through it with a huge smile on her lips.

"Finally, the big day has arrived..." My mother is proud. She married my cousin to my brother, and now it's my turn.

Zenda is a natural masterpiece, and it seems she wants everyone to follow her plans. It worked with me, but it didn't with my cousin. She wanted, at all costs, for Hassan to take Ayda as his second wife, blackmailing him, but it didn't work because Ayda married Abdul, my other brother. And now it's my turn, the damned marriage I tried so hard to avoid, the reality I didn't want to face.

I closed my eyes tightly, knowing I would have to give my body to another man again.

"The preparations are *in full swing* downstairs," I opened my eyes to see Malika stepping back as my mother came towards me. "Put a smile on that face, my daughter, you are marrying a Sheikh."

I forced a big smile on my lips, making Zenda roll her eyes. My mother ignores the fact that I am no longer a virgin, as if it were not a significant obstacle. For me, it is; my fiancé doesn't know I am no longer pure. In his mind, I am still a virgin, even though my sister-in-law asked me to tell him, I decided to make the more cowardly choice and not tell him.

What will his reaction be when he finds out? I don't know.

I won't bleed; I have already bled, been deceived, given myself to another man thinking it was for love, and was fooled. How can I believe in a man again?

"I will be able to tell everyone that I have a daughter living in the Agu Dhami palace!" I let out a long sigh as I heard my mother speak.

I walked around the room, heading towards the bed, sitting on it, holding my knee.

"Mom, I don't want to talk about how proud you are of this day, because I'm not..." I murmured with a tremor.

"Silly girl," Mom declared.

"If you want to stay downstairs helping with the reception, stay. I'll be here with Malika..." Zenda glanced sideways at my sister-in-law.

She doesn't like Mali; Mom hated her down to the last strand of hair when she found out my brother chose to stay married to just one woman.

"I don't trust her, I'd rather stay here," she shrugged, crossing her arms.

"Then, please, don't bring that contagious happiness to my side..." I said in a whisper.

Zenda went silent again, and soon the room was filled with women. My moment had arrived, the first day of my wedding...

FORTUNATELY, KHALIL didn't opt for many days of marriage; I can't stand keeping the smile on my lips any longer; the anxiety of the big moment is driving me crazy.

Perhaps it wasn't the best idea to leave the big revelation about my virginity for our wedding night.

What if he renounces me in front of everyone?

Not that I care much about that; after all, my life has never been normal.

Four men carry me on a throne suspended in the air, taking me to the big moment, towards my husband, to formalize the marriage.

THE SHEIKH'S FORBIDDEN BRIDE 9

They lower the throne. I keep my head down, and when I lift my face, I find it meeting an outstretched hand. I raise mine, with the entire palm painted with ink forming various designs and many jewels on my fingers.

I touch the man's hand; the warmth emanating from it makes mine feel warmer.

Khalil helps me down from the throne. He has a firm touch, wearing a well-fitted white suit, and his neatly trimmed black beard accentuates his face.

His brother, the ruler of Agu Dhami, stands beside him, while my brother, the governor of Budai, stands beside me.

I stand in front of my future husband, trying at all costs to avoid his gaze, a fact that might have caught his attention, as at some point Khalil raises his dark eyebrow, as if asking if I'm okay.

The truth is, I want to run away from there.

Our rings were exchanged, and the weight of that ring on my finger makes everything feel more real.

I am married. Married to a man I know nothing about. What am I supposed to talk to him about?

Khalil brings his face close to mine, his lips touching my forehead in a clear sign of respect.

"It seems that you are now my wife," he murmurs with his lips still on my forehead.

"Sorry..." I whisper, lifting my face and meeting his questioning gaze.

"Sorry for what, exactly?" His voice is low, deep, and somewhat husky.

A pleasant tone to listen to.

We are soon interrupted by men pulling Khalil by the arm, leading him to a group of men in a loud burst of laughter. It seems that there is no escape now...

CHAPTER TWO

Elahe

"How are you?" I turned my face to find my sister-in-law.

"Married?" I tried to find irony in my words.

"I thought Helena wouldn't extend the invitation to her family," Malika said with disgust.

"What's wrong with that?" I asked, curious.

"I'm not sure if I should tell you," Malika bit her lip, tormenting herself for having spoken too much.

"Just say it," I tried to be firm.

Hassan, my brother, interrupted us.

"Sister, how are you?" I think this is the most obvious question I've heard today.

"Fine," I looked at my sister-in-law, hoping she would continue what she was saying. But she changed the subject.

"Darling, I'm tired..." she looked at her husband, blinking a few times.

"Malika, I can't believe it," I gave her a disapproving look.

"The party is almost over; we can retire, especially since you're pregnant."

Malika must be about three or four months pregnant; her belly is still smooth. They both said goodbye to me, and I cursed my sister-in-law in her ear for starting to say something and not finishing it.

I looked around the hall again; a good number of people had already left. I spotted my mother's eyes coming in my direction, but I was intercepted by Helena first, my new sister-in-law.

"Hello, dear," she said in our language with a Portuguese accent.

I don't speak Portuguese, but I'm fluent in Spanish, and when I was practicing that language, I learned that some ways of speaking are similar. I've always liked studying, so I'm fluent in four languages, but no one needs to know. Dad always taught me that unless proven otherwise, no one needs to know everything about you.

I greeted Helena with a kiss on the cheek since we hadn't had the chance to talk yet.

"It will be so good to have a friend here; this is my sister," she pointed to a woman next to her. "Fernanda."

Helena spoke with her in her language, but I could understand what they were saying.

The woman looked me up and down. She is beautiful and looks nothing like Helena. Fernanda greeted me with a brief kiss on the cheek.

It was clear that the woman felt out of place, as if she didn't belong to any of this, but what bothered me most was the way she looked at me.

"Here you are," Fazza, the Emir of Agu Dhami, approached, standing behind his wife.

Out of the corner of my eye, I saw my husband approaching. His eyes were fixed on the other woman, Fernanda. Is it what I'm thinking?

"Has your brother retired?" Helena asked.

"Yes, Malika is tired."

"The early months of pregnancy can be tiring," the woman spoke again.

"Yes," I murmured, noticing that Khalil hadn't positioned himself close to me but rather in between me and the Brazilian woman.

I spent a few seconds analyzing the scene before turning my attention back to Helena, who noticed my gaze on the couple.

"I heard you went to college," Helena tried to divert my attention, as if covering for her brother.

"I did, but I don't think I'll be able to work in the field," I let a forced smile slip.

"What did you study?" Fazza asked, interested.

"Veterinary Medicine."

"Wild animals?" he asked, interrupting what I had just said.

"I heard you have two incredible lionesses," I smiled, seeing Helena huff.

"You're not going to tell me that you like that?" Helena asked.

"My father had one, but she was already old when she passed away. There was a vote, and everyone opted not to get another one, although I tried to persuade Hassan when he took over the palace, but it didn't work," I shrugged. "Well, now I have a horse."

"Quite similar!" the Emir joked. "I can take you to meet Aziz and Ali..."

"Argh..." Khalil cleared his throat. "Those things can bite you."

He made a funny face that made me smile.

"What doesn't kill you makes you stronger," I said directly to my husband, who raised an eyebrow at me.

"Tell me, what are you afraid of?" He was direct.

Khalil has a pleasant voice to listen to, rough and smooth.

I pondered for a moment, but the most obvious answer came to mind.

"I'm afraid of the truth..."

"Do you prefer the lie?" Khalil retorted.

"If the truth is painful, yes, I prefer it," he frowned questioningly.

"Sometimes the truth strengthens us. Better the truth than living a lie," he put his hand in the pocket of his white suit.

"Then I ask you, have you been truthful?" Instinctively, I looked at the Brazilian woman next to Helena, who was witnessing my heated conversation with Khalil.

I know he's hiding something about this woman; I saw the way he looked at her. I'm not a fool, and I wasn't born yesterday. I've always been a good observer.

Accepting this marriage hurt simply because he took me as his wife only to avoid tarnishing the reputation of my sister-in-law Malika, with whom he exchanged forbidden kisses before she married my brother.

And now here I am, being his second choice, which makes me realize that perhaps I'm not even the second, but the third. Since he didn't even bother to stand behind me.

Khalil doesn't answer me, which makes it obvious what the answer would be: He has, or had, an affair with this Brazilian woman. And perhaps it wasn't just kisses.

Fazza clears his throat in the face of the present silence.

"Why don't you two leave? You're the newlyweds; you must be tired," Fazza tried to lighten the mood.

"You're right," Khalil sighed.

I looked back at my husband; he directed his gaze at the woman, who returned it. Contrary to what I expected, she showed no reaction to him.

By *Allah*, what is happening?

My husband made a brief gesture for us to walk.

With a nod, I said goodbye to my brother-in-law, who would be responsible for announcing that the newlyweds had already retired, which is somewhat amusing. Does Khalil not want this marriage as much as I do? Did I marry a man who loves another woman?

And I thought I would only have to share his heart with my sister-in-law, whom he once loved.

What a mistaken notion I had!

How foolish I am!

CHAPTER THREE

Khalil

I open the door to my room for the woman to pass, or rather, for my wife. This all could have been different; it could have been her here, but Fernanda didn't want to live my life.

Under no circumstances could I be married to a woman who rejects all my customs. At first, it might have worked, as it did, but since nothing is ever smooth, arguments began to arise. Fernanda doesn't hold back on short clothes; she only respects when she's with her sister in Agu Dhami, but when she's elsewhere, she didn't even respect me.

Opposites may attract, but without respect, it will never work. We might have worked out for a short time, but in the long run, she wouldn't endure it, and I wouldn't tolerate seeing other men coveting what is mine. Fernanda was not meant to be mine; everything we had was good, but wrong.

That's why I'm married to her, Elahe, the perfect woman in the eyes of Arab society.

I begged Fernanda to reconsider, but she refused, practically insisting that I marry someone else, as she would never renounce her freedom for any man. Making it clear that she didn't love me enough to want to be by my side.

Perhaps Elahe is the more comfortable choice. Delicate, silent, always smiling. Although she has her own opinions, she was born to serve her husband, pure, and entirely mine.

I watch the young woman as she moves around my room, observing everything around her.

"This room has your scent," she murmurs, stopping in front of the window.

"And what would my scent be?" I ask in the silence of my room.

"It reminds me of the green smell of the forest, woody," Elahe doesn't look at me, observing the window through the thin curtain.

I walk toward her; it won't be difficult to have her in my arms. She's beautiful, of medium height, with brown eyes, a slightly upturned nose. What remains to be seen is the shade of her hair.

I position myself behind her.

I see her tense up, turning towards me, lifting her face.

"Is she your lover?" she asks directly.

I know she was smart enough to pick up on my hints.

"Who are we talking about?"

"Let's not be foolish," Elahe huffs impatiently.

I raise my hand, releasing the two pins that hold her hijab on her head. My fiancée doesn't move, her eyes fixed on me.

"Aren't you going to answer me?" she asks again.

"I thought you preferred lies..." I let out a forced smile.

"Not when the truth is thrown in my face."

I undo the hijab's ties, remove the scarf, and the veil that was with it falls to the ground.

"She's not my lover," I finally say.

I swallow hard as I see her hair cascade down her shoulders in long, dark waves, contrasting with her pale skin.

"But have you had something with her?"

"Do you want to discuss this on our wedding night?" I frown.

"I thought it would be humiliating enough to know that my husband only wanted this marriage to keep my sister-in-law from becoming the talk of the town, a woman he had an affair with. Now I discover that this humiliation wasn't enough, as in the line of succession, I am your third choice," Elahe lets out a forced laugh and avoids me, walking around the room.

"By *Allah!*" she slams her hand on her waist, "I need to get out of this stupid dress; it's suffocating me."

My wife holds the hem of her neck, not looking in my direction. I walk up to her again, positioning myself behind her. I unbutton one button at a time, without saying a word, knowing that an ill-timed word might make this woman explode with me.

When Elahe feels she no longer needs me, she steps away. I watch her slip the long dress off her shoulders, revealing her skin, then falling to her feet.

One foot at a time, wearing only a white, somewhat transparent nightgown, reflecting the weak light of the room on her curvaceous body.

"Why did you continue with this union when you clearly didn't want it?" Elahe asks again.

"Who said I didn't want it?" She lets out a long, sarcastic laugh.

"I must be a joke to you..."

"I don't know if you remember, but if we're here today, the main culprit is your mother..."

"My mother?" Elahe walks toward me. "Hassan made it very clear that he would find a way to prevent this marriage."

I am startled when her hand clenches into a fist and punches my chest.

I quickly grasp her wrist. Elahe lifts her head, her hair in her face, breathing heavily as she scrutinizes me with her eagle-like eyes.

"Your brother is a big fool who thinks he can solve everything," holding her wrists and pinning her to the bed, making the fabric of her nightgown bunch up between her thighs.

My wife is breathing heavily and looks at me terrified.

I place a knee on each side of her body. I lower myself over her, bringing my face close to hers, and whisper:

"Know that if you are here today, it was no coincidence. Decisions were made, and now you are my wife! You may be my first, second, or third choice; it doesn't matter, you are mine."

My eyes focus on her mouth, so small and full. Without giving her a chance to say anything, I bring our lips together.

The kiss is initially hard because she didn't want to yield. I persist until Elahe gives in.

My tongue enters her mouth, tasting her, sucking her lip, hearing a brief sigh escape her lips. I lower my hand along her waist, gripping the hem of her nightgown and lifting the fabric.

I bite her lip, hearing a groan of pain escape her mouth.

Supporting my hand on the bed, I stand up. I quickly remove my jacket, unbuttoning my shirt and pulling it out of my pants. I throw everything on the floor along with the jacket.

"Sit down," I murmur.

She doesn't comply. Her eyes are wide, fixed on my chest.

I huff, placing a knee on the bed, holding the hem of her nightgown. She has no choice but to sit. I can hear her heart pounding unevenly; her face brushes against my chest.

I slide the nightgown over her head, revealing her full breasts. Damn, I never imagined she could have such large and pointed breasts.

I lower my face and grab her hair, making her look at me. Her cheeks are flushed red with explicit embarrassment.

I lower my face, bringing my lips to hers, kissing her again, this time a slower kiss, savoring every corner of her mouth, lowering my lips. I appreciate every part of her neck, sucking on the pure skin of my wife.

I release my grip on her hair, pushing her toward the bed, moving toward her nipple, feeling her mounds in my hand, squeezing. I bring my mouth close and suck on the nipple, circling my tongue.

I lower my hand, pulling the delicate fabric of her panties, tearing them.

"Khalil..." my name escapes her lips in a plea.

I can feel my penis throbbing in my pants, incessantly demanding to be freed.

Elahe doesn't even touch me, which makes things more complicated, as all I want is her hand on my cock.

But I need to go slowly.

I stand up again, unbutton my pants, seeing her eyes fixed on my movements, pull down the fabric, along with my underwear, freeing my member. My eyes drop to my wife's naked body, her chest rising and falling rapidly. Her pussy so small and delicate, like a rosebud that I'm about to deflower.

Damn!

She is mine!

I may not love her, but she is mine.

"There's something I need to tell you," she says anxiously.

Her voice is weak, breathless.

"Can we leave that for later?" I ask, returning to position myself above her.

"Later might be too late," our eyes meet.

"Let's leave it for too late," I murmur, feeling my penis brush against her entrance. I lower my hand, feeling her warm pussy on my fingers.

"Ah... damn! You're so hot..."

I stimulate her entrance, lowering my lips to kiss her mouth.

When I realize she is surrendered to the act, I let my member touch its object of desire, penetrating her pussy.

Damn, she is so tight.

Elahe grips my arm tightly, her nails digging into my skin.

"Khalil..." she calls me again amidst the kiss.

I swallow her moans. Elahe remains tense, as if she urgently needs to say something.

I lift my face, slowing the rhythm of our movements.

"I'm not pure anymore..." she murmurs, "I won't bleed..."

Her words hit me like a punch to the stomach.

Knowing that I've been deceived all this time, I resume thrusting into her, this time more forcefully.

"Is this how you planned to tell me?" I frown.

"Sorry, I... I..." she bites her lip.

I let out a forced laugh.

"If you're no longer pure, then ride my cock," I demand this time, being somewhat harsh. I shift positions, watching how confused she looks when I put her on top of me.

"No, no, no... I'm not experienced, I... I..." she stumbles over her own words.

I position myself back on top of her, inserting my penis into her entrance, going deep, sliding my hand down to stimulate her pussy, hating the fact that another man has already touched her.

I need to relieve myself, damn it!

What a damn time for her to say this!

With all my strength, I have to control myself so as not to fuck her with excessive force.

"Why did you lie to me?" I ask, gripping her neck.

"I... I..." she can't speak.

I realize that amidst the torment, she is almost surrendering, and I let it happen.

Elahe rolls her eyes, her pussy writhing on my cock, which responds in kind, spilling deep inside this little liar. I let my body fall briefly on hers, but soon I pull away and stand up.

"You lied. And if there's one thing I don't forgive, it's lies! You can pack your things and go back to Budai with your brother," her eyes widen at my words.

"No, you can't..." she whispers.

"Did you want to hold something against me when you were lying yourself? I hope never to see you again!"

"You don't understand..." Elahe stands up.

"I don't want to understand! You lied, and that's reason enough. Get out of my sight!"

My disgust is so great that I just grab my clothes from the floor and put them on haphazardly.

How could I have thought she was the ideal woman?

CHAPTER FOUR

Elahe

A hole opens in my feet. The thing I feared the most has happened: he rejected me. I am alone in this room, staring into nothingness.

Acting on impulse, I head toward the closet, thankful to find my clothes there. I put on any tunic and grab a hijab to cover my head. Without thinking about what to do, I leave the room, needing to find my sister-in-law. I walk through various corridors until I find a servant and ask for directions, wanting to know which room my sister-in-law is in, knowing she is with my brother. The man points in the direction and I follow.

My eyes are blurry from the tears streaming down, as if I can still feel Khalil's hands on my body.

And I thought it would be as bad as it was with Ihab; what a mistake! I enjoyed it, but I didn't want to admit it to him.

By Allah! What was I thinking to tell him in this way? I stop in front of my brother's door. I begin to knock incessantly until I hear footsteps from inside the room. My brother opens the door.

Without giving him a chance to speak, I go straight in, not noticing the clothes they were wearing.

"Sister-in-law, what happened?" Malika gets up from her bed and comes toward me.

"He... he... rejected me," I murmur, accepting the embrace Malika gives me.

"I'm going to kill that bastard!" I hear Hassan's voice.

"Stay here, Hassan, let's hear what Elahe has to say," my sister-in-law holds my hand and leads me to her bed. "We were anxious about tonight, so we were waiting for you, sister-in-law."

Malika gets a glass of water and hands it to me, and I take long sips. My brother stands beside me, both of them well-dressed as if they had really been waiting for me.

"Tell us what happened. Did you consummate the marriage?" Hassan asks.

"I told him I was no longer pure... and yes, we consummated it. But he... he loves that other woman. He didn't even need to tell me, I could tell. And when I told him, he said we wouldn't be together anymore, and that I could go back to Budai with you. — I hold the glass with both hands.

"I'm going to kill him!" Hassan says, making Malika hold his hand to stop him.

"I don't want to! I don't want to be humiliated by men anymore, I don't want my fate decided by men, I want to escape..."

"How?" My brother cuts me off as if I were crazy.

"What do you have in mind, sister-in-law?" Malika sits next to me, holding my hands.

"I want to escape. Go to a place where no one knows me, another country, where there are no hierarchies like ours. I want to be an ordinary person among many others."

They both look at me, alarmed, with Hassan on the verge of rejecting my madness.

"Please, let me live my life. Help me escape! You don't have to say you helped me, just make this connection for me. In return, I will always keep you informed of my whereabouts..." I say in a plea.

I know my brother is struggling internally between his desire to act as a brother and his duty as the ruler of an emirate. Knowing that it is madness to flee from a husband in this way. Even though Khalil rejected me, he is still my husband.

"Please..." I beg.

"This is madness," Hassan runs his hand through his hair, pacing back and forth.

"And what if Khalil changes his mind tomorrow?" Mali asks.

"If he changes his mind, it will be too late; I'll be far away," I shrug.

"I can't agree with this madness. You are my sister, Elahe."

"If I don't do this with your help, I'll do it alone and it will be worse because you will never know anything about me," I say determinedly.

"Malika?" Hassan calls his wife, wanting to know her opinion.

"We will help you, sister-in-law."

I smile at her, thanking her silently.

"Where do you want to go?"

"Los Angeles. I speak English well, I want to live in Santa Monica. By the sea, have some business, something where I can blend in, where everyone will look and think I have a quiet life."

"I see you already have a completely mapped-out plan," my brother murmurs.

"It wasn't very difficult. I want to be far away, where no one will recognize me."

"Alright, we will arrange this now. Pack your things, I'll send a driver to pick you up and take you to Budai. From there, Abdul will be waiting for you; he will travel under the name of one of our employees so your name won't be registered with the airline. I will provide you with a card in my name, so nothing will be moved from yours. In return, I want to talk to you every day, sister."

"I admire your quick thinking, brother." I got up, leaving the glass on the table next to the bed.

I approached Hassan, hugging him, smelling the perfume I'm used to.

"We will never know anything, Elahe. If anyone asks us, you never informed us of anything," Hassan says with his chin touching my head.

"Thank you," I murmur.

"Now I need to call Abdul and keep him informed about everything."

"I didn't want to involve more people in all this," I say, pulling away from him.

"But it's necessary."

I turned my body, looking at my sister-in-law, receiving a tight hug from her.

"Knowing that you would be living here was already sad enough. Imagine living hours away from me? I will miss you so much," she murmurs. "I'm feeling guilty."

"Don't feel that way, ever. You gave me my freedom, Malika, even if it was in the wrong way, but you gave it to me."

We intertwine our hands.

I know I've built a strong friendship with Malika; our connection was immediate. She was the best thing that happened in my brother's life, my best friend and confidante.

"Promise me you'll send photos of that belly when it starts to grow?" I ask through my tears.

"I promise."

In the distance, I heard my brother's voice whispering on the phone.

"Everything will be alright," I let out a long sigh.

"Yes, it will..."

"I think I could love him," I let a smile slip out.

"I think so too. But if you are meant to be together, *Allah* will unite you again."

There, I once again charted my destiny. Fleeing from my husband, fleeing from all my responsibilities, could be the greatest madness I have ever committed. Knowing that when this hits the local newspapers, I will be front-page news. I hope it doesn't reflect where I am.

CHAPTER FIVE

Elahe

TWO YEARS LATER...

I lean on the counter, watching the local news, which has no new updates. I resume wiping the dark mahogany of the counter, which reflects the varnish. My heels echo on the floor as I walk back and forth.

I see that night is beginning to fall outside, and the light of the sign in the window starts to blink in colors, making it clear that there is a bar here.

"Are you leaving already?" I turn my face to hear Logan's voice, my only bartender.

"Yes, soon," I murmur. I let out a loud sigh.

"Existential crisis?" he asks with a half-smile.

"Maybe," I shrug.

Logan has been with me since I arrived in Los Angeles. He knocked on my bar's door when we were renovating, asking if I needed staff. It seems his company was just what I needed at that moment.

Hassan was furious when he found out my first employee was a man, but he never intervened, leaving me here alone to steer my own life.

Logan became my best friend and confidant. I never imagined finding such a close friendship with a man here.

There was never any sexual pleasure involved, even though he is a handsome, mysterious, *bad boy* with an attitude, but our friendship always took precedence. He lives nearby, my apartment neighbor, having lost his entire family in a car accident, and has been living around ever since. He says he works for sport and doesn't plan to spend the money his family left him; he believes it's all temporary.

During one of our moments of confession, he revealed that he has a degree in literature, that his parents were from New York's upper class, but after losing them in an accident, he decided to give everything up and live as lightly as he could.

"Thinking about him?" Logan asks, picking up a glass from the tray and filling it with amber-colored liquid.

"Sometimes I catch myself thinking about him," I let a forced smile appear on my lips.

Logan knows everything. He knows I'm married, knows that behind the nickname Ella, there is Elahe, the woman nobody here knows. In their minds, I'm just a woman who came seeking a better life, opening a little bar.

I could have opened any other business, but what would be better than a bar, where I could remain unnoticed by anyone from Budai and Agu Dhami? Who would imagine that Elahe, the Sheikha of Budai, would open a bar and live like an American, passing under everyone's radar?

"That man must still wonder where his crazy wife is," my friend takes a long sip of his whiskey and hands me the glass.

I hold the glass in my fingers, taking a sip of the drink, feeling it burn my throat as it goes down.

"He rejected me..." I place the glass on the counter.

"But you still think about him," Logan has never been one to sugarcoat his words.

"Of course I think about him. I wake up every day with a little version of him beside me. And when he starts asking about his father?" I resume walking around the bar, removing the chairs that are on the tables.

The place is small, not very flashy, and most of the people who frequent it are regulars. At first, most of the men hit on me, but that changed once my belly started to grow.

Hassan sent a larger amount of money when Rafiq was born, which allowed me to hire a nanny to help, and of course, Logan helped with the bar's workload.

Today is Monday, and on Mondays, we open only in the evening. On other days, we open in the afternoon. Since Logan is the one who works the night shift, he usually stays open until the last customer. He loves listening to the drunk conversations. My friend helps lower the chairs, and we switch the sign to "Open."

"You know he's going to want to know about his father, right?" Logan says as I take my place behind the bar with him.

We don't have many customers, so not many staff are needed. We manage well, just the two of us.

"May that day be delayed. He's only one year old..."

"And what about you? What if he sends a divorce request? By mail?" He lets out a wry smile.

"It's not that simple; it's complicated. I don't know if I'm ready to face Khalil. I made a mistake when I lied; he rejected me, and his words are etched in my memory."

"Honestly, your people are very strange. Who says they don't want to stay married just because the wife isn't a virgin?" Logan furrows his brow in a funny way.

I shake my head as I see our first customers coming in. Mr. Marcos is a Brazilian who lives in retirement in Santa Monica. He says Brazil is too small for him; sometimes he comes accompanied by his wife, but today he is alone.

"Hello, beautiful Ella," he winks an eye with a flirtatious smile.

"Good evening, Marcos," after asking so many times, I stopped calling him Mr.

"Luiza stayed at home, said she's preparing a sailor outfit for little Rafiq," the man reminds me of my son.

"Oh, we'll definitely love it!" I smile at him.

I see the bar starting to fill up, helping my friend with the first customers; I know everyone by name. When I notice that everything has started to stabilize, I head to the back of the bar, where our kitchen is located, grab my black leather jacket, as it's usually cold at this time with the sea breeze. By the reflection of the electric oven, I turn to check if my pants are dirty; the light jeans are tight on my body. I toss my hair back and hold my handbag.

At first, it was strange walking with my hair loose, but I needed it to go unnoticed, especially since my disappearance was making headlines across the Emirates.

The luck was that Logan covered for me most of the time, until my face was out of most of the spotlights. My brother kept his part of the deal by remaining silent about my disappearance.

I pass through the double doors, walking towards my friend who is filling a glass with some drink.

"I'm leaving, call me if you need anything," I wink at him as he lowers his face to give me a kiss on the cheek.

We say our goodbyes.

"Don't forget to bring what I asked you for, Ella," he says a little louder as I walk away, and I wave my hand in acknowledgment.

I step out from behind the bar, lost in my thoughts, missing my little boy, his toothless smile.

"Elahe?" My name echoes in the bar, that same voice I miss, the same voice that rejected me.

I turn my neck slowly, as if in slow motion, and there he is.

Materialized in my bar.

Khalil.

CHAPTER SIX

Khalil

HOURS EARLIER...

"What do you think?" Brayden asks, placing his hand in the pocket of his dress pants.

"It's a good investment," I shrug, looking at the sea in the background.

"Good? Seriously, Khalil? What world are you in?" my friend questions.

Brayden Zimmerman went to college with me; the bastard is taking over his father's company and is still thinking about new investments. If there's anyone more agile than this jerk, I don't know them.

Since we met at Harvard, we've never stopped talking. He lives in Los Angeles and invited me to be his partner in this new seaside inn he's planning, a few miles from the main street.

He brought me here to get a feel for Santa Monica beach.

"I keep looking at the sea, wondering how that woman vanished without a trace?"

"Think of it positively; that way, there's no hassle," my friend says, raising his arms and unbuttoning the first buttons of his shirt.

"Easy for you to say when I'm still legally married," I roll my eyes.

"Your culture is quite strange. Why did you reject her if you can't get her out of your mind?" Brayden looks at me confused.

"Elahe lied to me, which changes everything," I scoff.

"She lied about not being a virgin. Was she at least experienced?"

"No, not at all," I let the sentence die as I remember that day.

It may have been two years, but the image of Elahe doesn't leave my mind, of how I left her devastated, of how she tried to explain, but I didn't let her.

Damn it, she lied to me.

After that, I never saw her again. Hassan said she had gone to Budai, but when I went to fetch her, she was no longer there.

She simply vanished. I had the private jets of Hassan tracked, and none had made any suspicious trips; in his airline company, she wasn't seen on the cameras, of course, if she was wearing a hijab, she could have gone unnoticed at many moments. Her name wasn't in the company's records either.

Elahe took my command to flee literally. I might have said that in a moment of anger. But I would never reject her. Damn it, I have sisters, I know how much it could tarnish her.

But I did. And she vanished, tarnishing her image on her own.

As much as her brother says he knows nothing, I know he does. Malika didn't even look at me when I begged her to tell me where her sister-in-law was. It's impossible for someone to disappear like that. It's literally impossible.

I swear that if I ever find her, I'll lock her in a room just for the damn years she made me spend searching for her.

"You know you have a share of the blame in all this, right?" my friend interrupts my daydream.

"Why?" I want to hear his opinion.

"*Bro*, you didn't even let her explain herself. Have you considered that she might have been used, not to use a stronger word?"

Maybe he's right, since she barely touched me, always so withdrawn.

"How could that be possible? She was raised in a glass dome," I say, not believing this possibility.

"Even glass domes can break," Brayden shrugs.

I look back at the sea; could this have happened to her? Hassan was always so careful, how could something so careless happen to his sister?

I let out a long sigh. *Damn it!*

This silence frustrates me.

"Shall we go to that bar?" Brayden points with his finger.

I analyze the small place.

"Are you sure?" I raise an eyebrow.

"Yes, I've been there once. It looks simple from the outside, but it's cozy inside."

I check my wristwatch, seeing that it's already late and I need to go to the hotel. I promised Fernanda that I would call her. Perhaps after Elahe ran away, my relationship with her has become stronger, but not in a sexual way. Nanda said she doesn't want to be my mistress and refuses to end up in my bed. Not that I insisted; we just sat and talked about it, keeping our friendship a priority.

I think we were always meant to be friends; it just took us a while to realize that.

How can I lie in bed with another woman, knowing that the damn Elahe is out there, doing who knows what?

"Shall we go?" Brayden asks, crossing the street.

"Just one drink, I need to make a call," I grumble.

"Old grump," my friend punches my arm.

I analyze the glass that shows the interior of the place: everything in brown, rustic tones, with some people sitting at the tables scattered around the small space.

Brayden enters before me, the bell above the door jingles.

We make our way to the counter, where I sit on a stool next to my friend. A man works alone, serving the customers; he seems to be handling everything. He turns toward me.

"What can I get you today?" he asks in a casual tone.

"Two glasses of your strongest stuff," Brayden orders.

"Coming right up," the tall man turns around, facing away from us.

He doesn't have the look of a bartender; he seems like one of those bikers who rebel against life and end up in some small place.

The door next to him moves, revealing a woman passing through it. Brayden whistles beside me.

"Check out that body," my friend whispers beside me.

Indeed, the woman is worth admiring.

Her jeans hug her curves like a glove, revealing a shapely bottom, the heels making her taller, my eyes travel up to her leather jacket, giving her a wildcat style. Her black hair cascades over her shoulder.

She approaches the man, stands on tiptoe, and receives a kiss on the cheek. Amid her goodbye, she turns her face without seeing me, but I see her.

I could recognize that face anywhere.

By Allah, it's her! My wife, the damned wife of mine.

She moves out from behind the counter, and I quickly stand up, calling out the name of the woman who ran away from me.

"Elahe..."

As if the world stopped spinning, she turns her face, looking at me through a curtain of black hair.

Her terrified eyes lock onto mine.

My wife, the sweet Elahe, the innocent Elahe, has turned into an American woman.

Damn it, how dare she wear clothes like that for everyone to see what's mine!

I clench my fist, furious; I'm on the verge of dragging her by the hair and taking her to a locked room.

CHAPTER SEVEN

Elahe

Everything seems to stand still; before my eyes is him, the man from whom I fled.

How is he here?

Khalil hasn't changed at all; his intense, dark eyes are still the same. I need to think quickly. How can I escape him? I blink my eyes, hoping this is just a nightmare.

"Khalil..." I murmur his name, wishing to wake up, for the dream to end. But nothing happens; he's really here.

"Ella?" I turn my body to see my friend approaching. "Are you okay?"

Logan stops next to me, placing his hand on my back.

"Yes, she's fine. Get your damned hands off her!" Khalil growls at Logan.

"Hey, who do you think you are to speak like that?" Logan asks, practically positioning himself in front of me.

"I'm her damned husband, now get away from her!"

I lower my eyes, seeing Khalil with his hands clenched into fists.

"Hey, Arab, control your instincts," I see the man with golden hair approach, holding Khalil's shoulder. "Bro, it's not worth it..."

"Get your damned hands off her; I won't repeat myself," Khalil growls at Logan, ignoring his friend.

"Logan, I'm fine," I murmur to Logan, who is holding my arm. "You can go back to the counter."

"Are you sure?" He lowers his face, tucking a strand of my hair behind my ear.

I can hear Khalil growling like a caveman.

"I am," I wink at him, showing calm.

Logan has always been like a brother, and I know he doesn't understand how these mere touches in our culture can be considered inappropriate. He looks at Khalil, whom I'm sure is only standing still because his friend is firmly holding his shoulder.

"You can let go of Brayden," he declares, dodging the man.

Logan goes back to the counter.

"Friend, don't forget that we're not in the Emirates," Brayden runs his hand through his hair, pushing the short, blonde strands back.

Khalil doesn't say anything, just comes toward me, gripping my wrist tightly and pulling me out of the bar. His grip is firm, and to avoid drawing more attention, I go along without arguing, even though I grimace at the pain it's causing.

He keeps walking until we stop outside the bar, in a dead-end alley, where the light is dim, and I can only see part of his face from the reflection of the streetlights. Without saying a word, with the hand that's holding my wrist, he pushes me against the brick wall where I seek support to avoid falling.

"I swear..." he starts, running his hand through his hair furiously. "I swear I'm about to do something crazy!"

I don't say anything; perhaps it's better not to speak now. Khalil takes two steps forward, punching the wall next to my head. I widen my eyes, feeling my whole body tense. His face is close to mine; I can feel our breaths colliding, his chest rising and falling rapidly.

"Are you betraying me?" he asks, narrowing his eyes.

"Our commitment is only on paper," I gulp, feeling his body press mine against the wall.

"Our commitment is before Allah, before our family, and our people. Of all the situations, this is the one I least expected to find. Betrayal?"

He murmurs so low, coming out as a whisper, his face turning to the side as if he's plotting various ways to end me.

"You're a master at drawing your own conclusions. Think what you want," I don't lower my head.

I won't debase myself to him. This is different; we're not in Agu Dhami, it's been two years living alone, following my instincts. I won't allow myself to be humiliated again.

"That's what my eyes saw!"

"What did you see?" I spit the words.

"You and that man... you should throw her into the street of bitterness."

"Do it, Khalil! No one cares about that here; here it's different, here it's just me being me," I raise my hand, gripping his shirt tightly.

His eyes drop, staring at my gesture.

"I won't do it here; I'll do it in Agu Dhami, in front of everyone. I'll make you endure the humiliation you put me through when you left..."

"Humiliation? Really, are we talking about this?" I try to push against his hard chest, but it's impossible given his strength.

"Are you going to tell me you're innocent? You ran away, married without being pure, made everyone look at me with pity..."

"I'm not talking about affairs! I'm saying you have such a big ego that you don't even bother to listen to the other person's opinion! To know what she went through."

"Now that doesn't matter anymore, because I went to Budai... I went to get you, I was going to let you explain, and imagine my surprise when I found out you weren't there anymore?"

"You rejected me, made it clear you didn't want me anymore." The night breeze passes, making me draw in the air forcefully, smelling his perfume. That same feeling from before overtakes me.

Of all the men, Khalil was the only one who stirred something in me, making me want to go further, but his harsh words deeply hurt me.

"And now I'll do it in front of everyone, with our family as witnesses; you're coming back with me to Agu Dhami."

No, I can't go back there.

"We'll formalize our divorce, make it real; it's been two years, there's nothing left to bind us. I'll give you the divorce and you can go back to your quiet life." I feel a tinge of disappointment in his voice.

"I'm not going back to Agu Dhami..." I murmur.

He lets out a forced laugh, as if my opinion isn't worth considering.

"Just give me one reason. After all, we can't stay married if we don't even live as such..."

At that moment, his phone starts ringing. Just when I was about to reveal that we have a child. Khalil finally steps back, and I miss his presence.

I lower my gaze, watching him take the phone out of his pocket, the name Fernanda shining on the screen. He ignores the call. I remember that name; it's the Brazilian. He's still in contact with her, and if they're still together?

"Looks like I'm not the only one committing betrayal," I mock, stepping away from him.

"I don't owe you any explanations about that..."

"Great, that means I don't owe you any explanations either!"

"You're a damn stubborn woman! Is it possible you can't put your life on hold to come with me to Agu Dhami?"

"No, I don't want to go there... unless you know that..." I let the sentence trail off.

"Know what?"

Khalil runs his hand through his thick black hair.

"That we have a child," I murmur, letting the sentence die.

CHAPTER EIGHT

Khalil

A *child? A child? What do you mean?*
It's as if my neurons are short-circuiting; she hid a child from me?

"What are you talking about?" I ask, stunned.

"We have a child," Elahe repeats.

A child... It's as if every time she said that, it made no sense. *I have a child? A child with Elahe?*

This makes everything more complicated.

"You hid a child from me?" I'm in shock.

"Yes, I hid him," she confirms.

From the reflection of the night light, I see her biting her lip.

As if it wasn't enough that I wanted to kill that bastard for touching my wife, for seeing her smile at him.

"How? Why?" I shake my head, not understanding.

"I can't go back with you to Agu Dhami; it's not just my reputation at stake, but our child's..."

"A child I don't even know!" I mock in the midst of my despair.

"Do you want to meet him?" Elahe asks, and I can see she's uncomfortable.

"Yes, I do!" I reply with the obvious.

"Come on..." she gestures with her hand.

Her heels echo on the sidewalk, her long hair flowing gently with the night breeze. I follow her, grabbing my phone and sending a message to Brayden, telling him not to wait for me. Then I do the same for Nanda, informing her that something unexpected came up and I won't be able to call her.

And at the end of the message, I add that I've just found out I'm a father.

I lift my head, watching my wife walk ahead of me. I immediately remember Brayden whistling at her, the man touching her.

Damn it!

Elahe is mine, while we're married. She is mine; how dare she wear those clothes? I want to tear all those clothes apart.

"It's here," she points to a building that must be about four stories tall.

It's simple. Too simple for someone who came from wealth like her.

I don't say anything; I follow her as she pushes open a glass door, and I enter with her into a reception area.

Elahe climbs the stairs, and my eyes keep wandering down to her butt. *Damn tight jeans!*

Stopping in front of a door, she takes the key from her jacket pocket, unlocks it, and opens it.

"Maggie, I'm here," she says a bit loudly as she walks through the door.

I hear footsteps in the apartment.

"Ella, dear," the woman comes to my wife, giving her a kiss on the cheek. "Our little one is in the living room, playing with the blocks."

The short, chubby woman looks up at me, briefly widening her eyes.

"Oh, Maggie..." Elahe remembers I'm behind her. "This is Khalil, well, *uh*... he's my husband, Rafiq's father..."

"Oh, you're married!" The woman is as surprised as I am.

Rafiq, that's my son's name. Now he has a name: my boy, Rafiq.

"Yes, I am," Elahe seems embarrassed.

"This man looks like he walked out of a model magazine, one of those Arab magazines... look at that watch!" Maggie says loudly, as if she's rambling. "Oh my goodness! I know him! You're the man who was looking for his wife."

The woman puts her hand over her mouth.

"It would have been much more useful if I had found out sooner," I scoff.

"Are you his princess?" Maggie looks at Elahe.

"Actually, I'm not a princess; my father was a Sheikh, I'm a Sheikha," Elahe corrects the woman.

"Is that more important? Am I taking care of a little Sheikh?"

I let a smile escape in front of the woman, who is horrified by the reality that was right under her nose.

"Technically, yes..." Elahe lets the sentence trail off.

"And here I was wondering who would leave a man like him; this is too much, what madness," the woman shakes her head. "I need to go, Ella."

"Oh, Maggie. Please, for the sake of our friendship, don't tell anyone about this. If it gets out to the press, it will be chaos," my wife pleads with the woman.

"I won't tell anyone," Maggie takes my wife's hand. "Promise me you'll take me to see those fancy Emirates?"

I watch the smile that forms on Elahe's lips; she's such a beautiful yet irritating creature.

"I will, I'll ask Hassan to welcome you."

"Hassan is who?" she asks, not understanding.

"The most arrogant man in Budai," I complete.

"Don't pay attention, Hassan is my brother, the Emir of Budai."

"Like a king?" The woman's eyes sparkle.

"Yes, something like that," Elahe nods.

The little old lady leaves the apartment, radiant, but not before stopping by my side and sniffing me. Yes, she sniffed me.

"The smell of wealth, handsome man," she says to herself as she leaves.

"By Allah!" I murmur, shaking my head.

"Maggie is Rafiq's nanny. She might seem a bit crazy, but our son loves her," Elahe says as soon as we're alone.

"I was wondering how you could leave him with her; she sniffed me!" I frown.

"I don't judge her; Arab men are the most fragrant."

"Did you say that in the plural?" I clench my jaw.

"Yes..." she shrugs.

"I'm noting all of this down for when I put her on punishment," I murmur.

"You'd better have a good memory," Elahe tilts her head, being as haughty as she always is when we're in an argument.

"And on top of everything, she's audacious..." I walk toward her. But I stop when I hear a child's voice.

"Mama..." I freeze.

I turn my face toward the small room, which has only a sofa present. The place looks like a cubicle but is well-arranged, with high-end furniture. At least this comfort is for my son.

My eyes fix on the boy; his hair is messy, falling onto his forehead, his dark eyes, slanted to the side. Damn, the kid looks just like me. Not wanting to be modest, but he's my son, it's stamped on every feature.

Damn, I have a son, a kid.

It's hard to grasp, but he's mine. Just like his mother, she's mine.

If Elahe ever tried to run away from me, it won't happen again.

Even if I have to tie her to the foot of the bed.

"Hi, my little love," Elahe softens her voice, bending down to pick up our child.

I watch the scene, imagining what I've missed in these two years, what she took from me by running away. I'll make Elahe pay for every day she hid my son from me. Even if it's a payment in sex, she will pay!

CHAPTER NINE

Elahe

I hold Rafiq in my lap, my little boy with just two teeth. Can such a small being make us strong? I lift my face, meeting Khalil's eyes on us.

His expression is unreadable; I don't know what's going on in his mind.

"This is Rafiq..." I murmur, turning my son towards him.

He says nothing, just tilting his head briefly to the side, as if contemplating what to do.

"A child who you stole two years of my life with...," he whispers, his voice hoarse.

"I only found out about the pregnancy when I got here," I declare.

"That didn't stop you from telling me. He's my son too, just as much as he's yours. You took away my right to be his father," Khalil runs a hand through his furious hair. "What was my role in choosing his name? Where was I present? Damn it, Elahe, you had no right to take that from me!"

Khalil changes the tone of his voice and starts pacing back and forth, frightening Rafiq, who begins to cry in my lap. Amidst a puff of air, I leave him alone in the room and go to the kitchen with my little one.

"*Shh...*" I rock him in my arms, placing him in the high chair.

I hand him some toys.

Bending down, I stroke his chubby cheeks, calming his cries as he focuses on the toy car in his hand.

My son lifts his tear-streaked eyes and gives a toothless smile, making me melt a little more for him. It's hard to believe that this little thing came out of me. He may have all his father's traits, but he's as much mine as he is his.

I stand up, straightening my body. Rafiq starts rolling the toy car over the tray of the high chair, making small "brum, brum" sounds, letting drool escape from his mouth as he plays, captivated by his toy.

I look up and see Khalil entering my small kitchen. He's putting his phone back in his pocket.

I turn my back to him, looking for something to eat. Usually, Maggie leaves something; she always makes sure Rafiq is fed and ready to sleep. Sometimes, when the little one is restless, he ends up eating a second time with me.

"If you plan to change your tone of voice again, you'd better leave, or do you want Rafiq to have a good first impression of his father?"

"I bet he doesn't know what that is," he mocks.

"He might not know, but he records people's faces," I glance over my shoulder.

I unzip my jacket, taking it off and leaving it on a piece of furniture.

"I haven't changed my mind about you coming back to Agu Dhami with me," he says, grabbing my attention as he pulls out a chair and sits down next to Rafiq.

The boy lifts his eyes and happily offers the toy car to the man beside him.

"What makes you think I'll go back?"

"Rafiq..." he says the name that would make me go to the moon. "For me?"

Khalil focuses his attention on our son, taking the toy car in his fingers, playing with the boy in the high chair, pushing the toy around.

"I'm not going back to Agu Dhami," I murmur.

THE SHEIKH'S FORBIDDEN BRIDE 43

"You will, unless you want to be without him," Khalil doesn't even look at me, concentrating on our son.

"I wouldn't dare do that," I walk toward him.

"Not only would you dare, but I've already informed Fazza that I'm coming back tomorrow with you and our son," the man doesn't look at me.

"I'm not going!" I stamp my feet determinedly.

"How about getting to know the coolest place, son?" he says in a loving tone to our child.

Rafiq claps his hands, not understanding what his father is saying to him. Khalil smiles at the boy. Even smiling, they share the same features.

"See? He's on board," at that moment Khalil lifts his eyes towards me, focusing on the neckline of my shirt. "An extra detail for your punishment, that damned neckline."

"He's just a one-year-old baby; do you think he understands anything?" I cross my arms.

"Whether he does or not, you two are coming with me to Agu Dhami, and you won't leave my sight until I trust you," he lets go of the toy, leaving Rafiq to play on his own.

"I thought you were going to deny me in front of everyone," I raise an eyebrow.

He stands up, passing in front of our son's chair, coming toward me. I take a step back, hitting the kitchen counter, my eyes widening at his intimidating expression.

"I would have done that, before knowing about his existence. Now you two will be mine. Unless I decide otherwise, of course, this only applies to you, since he is my son."

"I'm not like property," I murmur, shaking my head.

"You've been mine since you signed the marriage contract. Accept it, because I won't grant you freedom. Starting tomorrow, I want you covering your hair, wearing modest clothes. You're mine! Was I clear enough?"

"You've denied me..."

"Not in front of witnesses, so it's your word against mine. We have a child, and he will be the bond that ties us together. You'll come with me, and that's final!"

Khalil presses his body against mine again, his masculine scent filling my senses. I narrow my eyes, glaring at him, cursing fate for putting me in his path.

"And what if I don't go?"

"I'll take our son from you, and you know I can do it!" He clenches his jaws, seething with anger towards me.

"You wouldn't dare..." I whisper, unable to believe it.

"Believe it, I'd even do worse!" He tilts his head slightly, scaring me even more.

I release a long sigh, realizing I had been holding my breath.

"Tell me, Elahe, that man from the bar, what is he to you?"

Khalil clenches his jaw so tightly that I can see it twitching along his beard.

"Logan? As much as you want to hear that he's my lover, you're mistaken. We've always been just friends. If anyone betrayed me these past two years, it was you, and apparently, you're still doing it..." I refer to his friend.

"It seems we're even then," he lets a smile appear.

"I don't believe you..."

"Just as I don't believe you, I guess we're in the same boat on that," he shrugs.

"*Mamma...*" Rafiq babbles my name.

I almost thanked him, as it made me escape from his father's touches.

By Allah, how can he still have the same effect on me?

CHAPTER TEN

Elahe

I straighten my body over Rafiq's crib, grabbing his bottle from the side of the crib. I turn around, meeting Khalil's eyes, which are fixed on our son sleeping peacefully. He raises his hand, scratching his beard.

I walk towards him, brushing past him. I head to the kitchen, where I wash Rafiq's bottle and place it on the counter.

I hear Khalil's footsteps dragging. I turn my body, meeting him.

"I can't go with you tomorrow; I have business here," I say, drying my hand with a towel.

"I don't care; you're coming with me. None of this matters."

"Khalil..." I say his name in a sigh.

"It's no use, Elahe. I've been deceived by you once; twice would be too foolish."

"I give you my word that I will. Just give me a few days to say goodbye..."

"A few? No, I won't give you any..."

"Please?" I ask softly, leaving the cloth on the counter.

"No! You're coming with me, tomorrow!"

He's adamant, his hawk-like eyes glaring at me with the anger he feels towards me.

"Why? Why did you lie to me? Why didn't you say you weren't a virgin anymore?"

"I don't want to talk about it. If you don't trust my words, talking or not talking about the truth right now won't make any difference," I huff, heading to my room.

My room is next to my son's.

I enter, heading straight for the bathroom. I can hear Khalil's footsteps coming towards me, and from the corner of my eye, I see him enter the room.

"I'm going to take a shower. Don't worry, I won't run away," I stop, holding the bathroom door handle. Khalil says nothing, just scratches his beard, leaning against the door frame of the room.

I enter the bathroom, lock the door, tie my hair in a bun on top of my head, and remove my clothes, leaving them on the laundry basket.

I turn on the shower, lathering my whole body, letting the water run over every part of me, tired and exhausted from fighting with him.

Who could have imagined that one more normal day could become the most tumultuous in two years? I, who never imagined I'd see this man again. I turn off the shower, stepping out of the shower, grabbing a robe, and tying it around my body without even drying myself properly. Dragging my feet on the floor, I leave the bathroom, my eyes going straight to the door where he was before.

"Are you looking for me?" I turn my face quickly, finding him standing by the bathroom door. If his expression was anger before, now it's something completely unreadable.

"You scared me," I murmur.

"I'm furious, irritated with you, and all I want to do right now is punish you, every day, for two years, for all the time you made me search for you, for hiding a child from me, for lying..."

I gulp when he grabs my hand tightly, walking me to the bed, pulling me and throwing me in the middle of it. The robe, which isn't tied properly, opens up. I try to close it, but Khalil is quicker, removing the belt from his pants, pulling it fast, kneeling over me, raising his hands, grabbing mine, pulling them above my head, and tying both my wrists.

"What are you doing?" I ask, terrified.

"What I wanted to do since I saw you in that damn bar, kissing another man on the cheek, wearing those hellish jeans," he roars the words. "You signed a marriage contract, which meant you'd be mine forever, and you broke it, showing yourself to the world, and I'm furious."

I feel like a doll at his mercy, I tried to struggle, but my strength is nothing compared to his. Unable to move, he sits on the bed, turning me around, making me lie on his lap, my backside raised on his lap, my face on the pillow.

Holding my legs, he delivers the first slap to my backside, echoing in the silent room.

"By *Allah*, are you out of your mind?" I ask, turning my face to the side.

Khalil doesn't stop, giving another slap to my backside, followed by another.

The slaps are painful, as if he's venting all his anger there.

Even as I beg, he doesn't stop, his breathing is rapid.

"Repeat it for me, or I won't stop..." he says, stroking my backside, my sensitive skin. "You're my wife...."

I don't speak immediately, which makes him slap me again.

" *Ouch*...," I complain. "Yes, yes... I'm your wife."

"Say it again!" he demands, delivering another slap.

"Damn it! I'm yours, yours, please, stop now..." I plead in a desperate voice.

"Know that this isn't over, but for now, I'll give you a break," Khalil starts to stroke my backside.

His hand descends between my wet backside, so damp it leaves me confused.

"Did you enjoy getting a spanking, wife?" he mocks, running his finger towards my intimate area, which hasn't been touched in a long time.

"Let me go," I plead, not responding to him.

Of course, Khalil doesn't do as I ask. He turns me on the bed, positioning himself on his knees.

"Tomorrow you'll spend the day remembering the wrong decision you made by running away from me. Your backside will remind you," he spreads my legs, and I try to close them, without success.

"Bastard, let me go!" I huff, staring at the ceiling, my hands aching from the belt that tightens around them.

"First, I need to taste something that has haunted me for two years. Your flavor..." he says, lowering his face.

I widen my eyes as he goes straight for my pussy, taking it into his mouth.

I feel his tongue there, licking me, moving up and down through my intimacy.

His tongue flicks against my pussy, echoing in the room. His skilled fingers reach my entrance, making me bite my lip hard, trying to deny the pleasure he's giving me. But it's impossible; a first moan escapes. Khalil smiles into my pussy.

"I know you want to resist, but your little pussy missed me..." he says with dirty words.

"Damn, I hate you!" I murmur amidst the ecstasy.

"Give in, come in my mouth, let me revel in your nectar..." he asks.

And it was impossible to hold back. I threw my head back as he sucked me fiercely, wanting to free my hands without success. I close my eyes, letting the delicious wave wash over every part of my body. How did I end up here? From hatred to having him between my legs, taking me in his mouth. Khalil stands up, and I'm sprawled on the bed, my body light, my buttocks sore. He comes to my head and releases the belt from my hands.

"Know that I'm still furious with you," he says, his face close to mine.

He wipes his beard, cleaning the luminous fluid there.

"Not more than I am. Don't try to blame me when it was you who rejected me..." he smiles at my words.

"Funny, because the only one who will be punished is you, and exclusively you. I wanted to fuck you hard, so brutally that you'd forget the damn decision you made to run away from me for a few years..." he roars, straightening his body with his belt in his hand.

"Bastard..." he lets out a forced laugh.

"Sleep, know that I won't be leaving this room tonight, so don't even think about planning anything. I'm going to make a call, and I won't take my eyes off this bed."

"I'm not a prisoner," I try to get up.

"Now you will be, mine..."

He turns his back and leaves the room. I'm left alone, thinking about what I got myself into by running away from him. Khalil is out of control with his anger towards me.

CHAPTER ELEVEN

Elahe

Damn Khalil for leaving me with this immense pain in my butt. I'm about to curse him to death. I woke up in the morning and thought he might have left, until I heard our baby's faint voice. I go over and find Rafiq in his lap.

"Why didn't you call me?" I murmur, closing my robe.

His eyes rise from the baby, coming towards me like an eagle.

"He didn't call you, so..." he shrugs as if it were normal.

I huff at his presumptuousness.

"I'm going to prepare his bottle," I say, turning my back and leaving him with the baby in his lap.

I wonder where Khalil stayed overnight until I see a laptop on the coffee table in the living room. Did he not sleep?

I enter the kitchen and prepare Rafiq's bottle.

I always wanted to breastfeed my child, but it was impossible; my milk just wouldn't come in, so I had to use a bottle. It was very painful for me at the time.

After finishing the preparation, I return to my son's room, where I find him sitting on Khalil's lap, drooling on his clothes while his father plays with him.

Both are in the armchair, my son, that little trickster, smiles at his father, who makes hand gestures. It could be a beautiful scene if it weren't for the current situation.

"I need to change his diaper," I declare, going over to them and leaving the bottle by the baby's dresser.

Khalil doesn't say anything, just hands me our child. It's at this moment that I realize he's not wearing the same clothes from the previous night.

He's in a burnt yellow suit, or rather, dress pants and a white shirt with the top buttons undone, revealing part of his smooth chest.

I lay Rafiq on the changing table, removing his clothes, playing with him in the process, changing his diaper, and finally putting on a clean outfit.

"All done, little snowflake," I joke with him, helping him to stand by holding his chubby little hands.

"Why little snowflake?" Khalil asks from my side.

"Because he loves watching a show that's about a little snowflake."

"Me... — Rafiq babbled, asking for the bottle.

I picked him up, who practically threw himself at me, sat in the armchair, being scrutinized by Khalil, who handed me the bottle. I laid Rafiq on my lap, leaving his little head slightly raised. The boy held the bottle with his tiny fingers, drinking by himself.

"He didn't wake up at all during the night," Khalil says.

"He hasn't woken up for a few months. In the first months of life, he woke up constantly. I spent some sleepless nights, but we adjusted over time."

"Was it just you two?" I raise my face to see him crossing his arms, leaning against the dresser.

"Yes, during the day Maggie came to help. She's a neighbor in the building, and she always helped me a lot," I mention, though I also had Logan's help, I prefer to omit that part to avoid another night of spankings.

I look back down, seeing Rafiq kicking his little feet as he drinks from the bottle.

"Where did you spend the night?" I ask without looking at him.

"On the sofa, working."
"Didn't you sleep?"
"No!" he responds curtly.

He remains silent but soon speaks again.

"We're going to Agu Dhami today; the jet is already waiting for us," he says, as I lift my eyes.

"And what about my things?"

"Write down what you need, and someone will come by to pick it up later..." He comes towards me and takes our child from my lap, as he's finished drinking the liquid.

Khalil takes Rafiq to the living room, avoiding eye contact with me.

I go to my room, knowing I'll need to wear some of my tunics. I only have two. I hold the burgundy fabric with black details, which covers all parts of my body. I change clothes, removing my pajamas. I find it strange to see myself in the mirror; it's been two years since I wore these garments, two years categorizing myself as something I'm not.

I love my culture; I've never stopped following my Muslim religion, I just adapted to the American style, trying to blend in as much as possible.

The tunic reaches my feet as I fasten the buttons at my neck, the light fabric fitting well on my body.

I hear the doorbell ring, I leave my room and go to the door, not without first checking Khalil with Rafiq in the living room.

I open the door to see my friend standing there.

"If Muhammad won't go to the mountain, the mountain will come to him," he winks.

"Logan," I take a step back when I realize he wanted to kiss my cheek.

Out of the corner of my eye, I notice Khalil's attention on us. I make a face at my friend, who understands the message.

"Come in," I invite him.

Logan removes his sneakers at the door, knowing that I hate it when people enter my home with shoes on.

"Hey, you crazy kid!" Logan jokes with Rafiq, who was in the living room with his toys, going over to his uncle.

"Uncle..." Rafiq babbles.

My friend picks up Rafiq, which makes Khalil get up from the sofa, letting out a growl.

"Uncle doesn't want trouble," he laughs, giving a kiss on my son's cheek and putting him back on the floor.

Rafiq returns to his father's side, his chubby little legs walking around the apartment.

Khalil sits back down.

"Logan," I ask him with a sigh, "I'm going back to Agu Dhami. I'll need you to take care of the bar alone. Hire someone to help."

My friend crosses his arms, raising one of his dark eyebrows.

"Are you sure?"

"Yes, she's sure," Khalil responds.

"Yes, I am," I confirm as well, knowing I have no choice. "Can you also let Maggie know?"

"Yes, I'll let her know."

"Thanks. Have you heard from your father?" I ask, knowing that his father was on the brink of death.

"No, I'll know when he dies," he shrugs as if it were no big deal.

"He's your father," I sigh.

"My progenitor, which makes everything different," he shrugs his shoulders.

"You've already lost your mother, your sister, and your stepfather."

"He was my father, this other one is not..."

"But you will inherit all your father's estate," I interject.

"I'll donate it to the first beggar I find..."

"You're impossible. Have I told you that?"

"Yes, I know," Logan turns his face towards Khalil. "If I find out that you mistreated her, I'll come to your Emirate and deal with you."

Khalil lets out a sarcastic smile.

"Try it..." my husband knows it's impossible to reach him when we're in Agu Dhami, not with the amount of security they have there.

"So, is this a see you soon?" he says just to provoke Khalil.

I shake my head, and before I have a chance to stop him, he gives me a hug. This act is followed by Khalil getting up from the sofa.

"Keep your filthy hands off her," I move away from my friend, seeing my husband standing beside me.

"Brother, you're so possessive; it's just a hug," Khalil growls at Logan's words, taking a step towards him.

"I'll smash your face if you touch my wife again, do you hear me? Want me to repeat it? I think not, even my son would understand that faster," he stops in front of Logan, almost ready to punch him. My friend, who isn't afraid of danger, lets a mocking smile escape his lips.

"You'd better take care of her, or she might run away again, and I'll be here to console her as the good friend I am," Logan says, pressing his face close to Khalil's.

They are both tall; Khalil is more built, but Logan works out a lot. This is a fight I don't want to witness.

"Enough, both of you..." I plead desperately, going to them and placing my hands on their chests to separate them. "Rafiq is over there, watching everything, terrified."

Khalil was quicker and pulled me by the wrist, making it clear that I am his property.

"I'm going now, Ella. Don't forget to call me," Logan winks as he leaves the apartment.

"You're not going to maintain a friendship with a man!" Khalil growls.

CHAPTER TWELVE

Elahe

The jet finally takes off.

I stay restless, constantly looking out the window. I haven't informed my brother that I'm coming back yet.

"There's no way we can pass unnoticed by the press, right?" I turn my face, finding my husband in his imposing stance.

"For you, or for our son?" he asks, directing his gaze at Rafiq, who is beside me, chewing on a toy.

"Especially for our son," I reply.

"For him, yes. I even requested that the jet land at the most distant helipad so we can go to the main palace by car without being noticed."

"Thank you," I say.

"No need to thank me; if it weren't for him, I wouldn't worry about the scandal..."

"But even so, you want me back by your side as your wife," I don't let him finish.

"It's different. I want you to suffer everything I went through in these two years of searching for you," he picks up the glass of whisky that was just served.

"I doubt that took up a significant part of your routine during that time," no drink was offered to me.

So I stretch out on the seat and grab the glass from his hand.

"Drinking like a man now?" He raises an eyebrow.

"Where does it say that this is a man's drink?" I ask, turning the glass in my hand.

I bring it to my lips, taking a small sip, feeling the liquid burn down my throat. I make a brief grimace and then take another sip, this time a little more adjusted to the taste.

"It seems you're resistant to alcohol. Lots of practice?" Khalil asks as I hand him the glass.

"Maybe," I shrug.

"Always with empty answers..."

"How am I supposed to give you something concrete when you don't believe me?" I question.

"Can I give you that vote of confidence?" he asks, as if he wants to know if he can trust me.

"If you give me the same vote..." I let the sentence trail off as Rafiq lets out a loud yawn beside me.

"Is he sleepy?" Khalil asks, and I nod. "Can I hold him?"

He asked, and I let him. Maybe it's easier for the baby to sleep on his father's broad chest than on mine, given the uncomfortable environment.

Khalil stands up, leaving the glass on the table between the two armchairs.

He takes Rafiq in his arms, sits down next to me, and our son yawns again, clinging to his father's chest.

He's all awkward, so I lean over, helping to make Rafiq lie comfortably on his chest. My hand touches his, sending a tingling sensation through my body. It reminds me of where that hand was last night, hitting my butt, entering my pussy.

Oh, heavens...

I blink, dazed, straightening up in my armchair. Khalil notices my discomfort and lets out a low chuckle.

"Memories, wife?" he mocks.

"Unpleasant memories..."

"That's not what it seemed like just now."

"You're so conceited, did you know that?" I turn my face. I'm leaning against the armchair, looking at him, who keeps his hands on Rafiq's back, who is playing with the button of his father's shirt, blinking his eyes as if he's fighting off sleep.

"I'm just speaking the truth. The truth is that you enjoyed getting spanked," his hand moves up and down the baby's back, soothing him.

"Who guarantees you that?"

"Your reaction, your body, everything about you gives it away. And know that your punishment isn't over yet. From 0 to 10, what's the level of pain in your ass? Don't lie!"

I shift slightly in my seat, feeling that discomfort, remembering his hand spanking my butt, and the worst part is that somehow, I liked it.

"Tell me, Elahe!" he asks impatiently.

"Maybe a 7," I finally declare.

"That's good, but not great. I'll have to increase it..."

"No! Are you crazy?"

"I'm going to fuck your little ass," he says, widening my eyes with his whisper. "With that, you'll spend a week unable to sit properly."

"I won't allow it..."

"That's what we'll see," he smiles that devilish smile, wanting to punish me at all costs for having run away from him. "You'll like it, like a good submissive wife, you'll like it and ask for more."

"I will never be submissive to you!"

"Nothing that a little psychological pressure can't resolve," he lowers his gaze to our son, knowing he can always use Rafiq to manipulate me.

"Please, Khalil, don't do this," I plead.

"Dear Elahe, let me remind you of something, you are not in a position to ask for anything!" His eyes narrow at me, making it clear that my plea will not be granted.

"When will all of this end?"

"When I get tired? When I give in that everything you made me go through, you went through twice as much?"

"If only you hadn't rejected me that day," I shake my head, not believing all that we're going through.

"If only you hadn't lied about your virginity, maybe I would have spared you. You know, Elahe, I would have accepted you without your purity, but you chose the easier path, starting a marriage based on lies... I hate lies!"

"You lied, you loved someone else," I declare, keeping my guard up.

"I could have loved someone else, but I knew my duties as a husband. I would be faithful to you, and only you. My affair with her was over, we had put an end to it. You were my fresh start, the ideal wife, who would follow all the steps without any scandal. How foolish I was..." Khalil loses himself in his thoughts. "Me, who always wanted to avoid scandals."

I had nothing to say in response. How could he draw all these conclusions about me? How did he come to think I could be the ideal wife? It seems that out of all his judgments about my actions, the path this took was by far the darkest, drawing his own conclusions about what he thought was best.

"Lost for words, aren't you?"

"I hate having expectations placed on me. What you did was wrong. I'm not perfect; you idealized something wrong, and given all this, the fall was great. Now you plan to take it all out on me."

"And I will, my dear, you can bet on it, I will..." Khalil murmurs as if it were a sentence for me.

"I hate you!"

"That doesn't matter. I have the most sordid plans for you..."

"Damn you!" I roar.

"Keep it up, and all it will do is make me increase the doses," I jump when his free hand goes to my thigh, squeezing it hard. "That hug with that man has already been added. No male should touch you. You are mine, only mine, Elahe!"

"Logan is my friend, just a friend!" I declare.

"Fuck that. This will serve as a lesson."

"By Allah!" I throw my head back.

"You might as well ask him a lot. You'll need it."

And after that, I was ignored, completely ignored for the rest of the trip.

CHAPTER THIRTEEN

Elahe

I swallow hard, watching the car stop in front of the Agu Dhami palace. Khalil beside me doesn't even care about my nervousness.

When we landed in Agu Dhami, I sent a brief message to my brother letting him know I was back in the Emirate with my husband, asking him not to interfere and that I would call when I could. One of the Sheikh's men opens my door, and I'm forced to get out.

I would have preferred to have Rafiq in my lap so I could have something to hide behind. But he's with Khalil, I know he's doing this just so I have to enter the palace alone, beside him. I wait for Khalil to go around the car and come toward me.

"Let's go," is all he says in our familiar language.

It's so strange to be speaking Arabic again. The palace remains the same, with its enormous walls and everything adorned with golden details. Rafiq, in Khalil's arms, continues to admire everything as if he's enchanted. If only he knew the mess I've gotten him into. I can feel curious and discreet eyes on me. My husband walks beside me, and we leave our shoes at the door. I'm so nervous that I can hardly breathe.

The doors to a room are opened, and I remember it being the main hall, where everyone usually gathers. There are two men, one on each side of the door, and I can hear muffled voices coming from inside the room.

"You will enter by my side," Khalil murmurs.

Another humiliation to add to my endless list of humiliations. I don't say anything, just continue walking beside him.

Swallowing hard, I enter beside my husband, unable to ignore the numerous glances in our direction.

No one says anything; the most that can be heard are loud "*ohs*."

"Brother," Fazza is the first to speak, breaking the silence.

He stands up from his imposing chair, his eyes don't even glance in my direction. It's clear how unwelcome I am in this place. Even Helena, the wife of the ruler of Agu Dhami, looks at me with disdain.

"When you spoke, I could hardly believe it," Fazza stands in front of his brother. Both are tall, though Fazza's demeanor is more serious, while Khalil usually shows more calmness.

"I still don't believe it, let alone you who are far away?" Khalil mocks.

"When will you make the announcement?" The emir is direct.

"For now, there will be no announcement," Khalil replies to his brother.

At this moment, Rafiq babbles, drawing the attention of the uncle who looks at him with disdain.

"Shouldn't you test this child as your own? Did you do any testing?" I narrow my eyes towards the emir.

I know he is being cautious with his brother, who is angry with me for running away, but no one speaks ill of my child.

"I don't think it's necessary, just look at his features," Khalil retorts to his brother.

"True, but you shouldn't fully trust her. After all, it's been two years, two years during which we know nothing about her," at this moment, Fazza lets his eyes fall on me.

Looking at me with disdain, reducing me to the worst kind of insect.

"Until I decide otherwise, there will be no announcement, and no one will treat Rafiq as a bastard. He is my son, and if that makes you more comfortable, we can do the test," well, at least at this moment Khalil wasn't a complete jerk. At least when it comes to Rafiq, he protects him.

"Always letting yourself be influenced by the ways of foreigners. At least uphold our culture, brother," Fazza snorts.

"And who says I don't?"

"Then reject her. Send this woman away from you. Don't you see that this only puts our family back in the news?" Fazza is starting to lose patience, and doesn't even care that I'm here, right beside them, with all the guests, making it clear that he doesn't want me in this palace.

What a warm welcome.

"I think I made it clear when I said I wasn't going to reject her. This isn't open for discussion. Rest assured, brother, my problems won't spill over onto you..."

"They always do! Not just onto me, but onto all of us, your family, all because you never think collectively."

"Did you think collectively when you brought a Brazilian into our family?" Khalil touches on his brother's weak spot.

From the corner of my eye, I see Helena getting up. I think she noticed that the atmosphere is starting to get tense between the brothers.

"Let him be, dear. Khalil is taking the best approach, the one he deems convenient for his life. Let's just support him as we always have," her sweet voice prevails in the room as she stands beside Fazza, not looking in my direction.

"My problems are nothing compared to yours. Always involved in scandals, debauchery. Just when I thought things would settle down, that we had found the right wife, another mess happens. By *Allah*!" The emir slams his hands on his waist.

"Want to compare now? Will this argument never end?"

"Enough, both of you!" I hear a lady approaching, recognizing her as Fazza's mother. "If you want to discuss grievances, go somewhere private. Khalil, you've been very irresponsible, once again. Lâmia will arrive tonight from her trip. I want to see her lay hands on your head about this."

Lâmia is Khalil's mother; I met her briefly at my wedding, and the woman in front of us, if I'm not mistaken, is Aiyra, Fazza's mother, who everyone knows was never in favor of Helena as Fazza's wife. Everything changed when she brought the first two sons for the Sheikh.

Khalil snorts beside me, as if he can't believe all this.

"Look, really, I expected more from my family," he murmurs, clearly irritated.

"We also expected you to be more sensible," Fazza retorts.

"Maybe it's time for me to leave this palace," I almost sigh with relief.

"No one will leave this palace!" Fazza orders.

"Then accept my son and my wife. That was the decision I made."

The entire room fell silent, as if they couldn't believe everything he was doing for the woman who abandoned him for two years. I know that behind all of this, there's a Khalil who just wants to take revenge on me, but in front of his family, he said nothing. I know when to speak and when to remain silent, and right now, the ideal is to stay quiet, when all I want is to get my child out of this circus since he's not to blame.

"If that's what you want, everyone in this palace will accept her," the emir finally looks me in the face "Welcome, Sheikha Elahe."

It was strange to hear someone addressing me by my birth title. He was merely polite, in front of his brother, because obviously, deep down, I am not welcome here.

But for my son, I'll have to endure it.

CHAPTER FOURTEEN

Khalil

"Brother?" I lift my eyes towards Fazza.
"Can we have a talk in my office?"
"What's the point in saying no?" I ask, rolling my eyes.
"You know I won't, come on!"
He motions with his head for me to follow. Elahe went to the bedroom; the trip was exhausting, and she and Rafiq are tired. And let's be honest, their reception wasn't the best. I'm on the verge of taking my wife and child and leaving this palace. Hatred consumes me when Fazza dismisses them.

Only I can punish her; their role is just to accept my wife! Simple and straightforward. Only I can feel this sting.

The emir might be the ruler of this Emirate, but above all, he is my brother, my family. But Elahe and Rafiq are also my family, and by Allah, I don't want her out of my sight. I'm here following Fazza's steps when I actually want to be monitoring even her breathing.

I climb each flight of stairs, anticipating a brief lecture from my brother. I've barely arrived in Agu Dhami, and he already wants to monitor all my movements. It's always been this way; I don't know how Fazza doesn't tire of trying without effect.

It was the same with Fernanda. He wanted me to break everything off, and well, he succeeded, but I made that decision with her. Nanda can't accept our culture; she was born to be free. I confess I considered abandoning everything and living with her, but that would never work. Elahe seemed like the right choice. That was until I discovered her lie.

Fazza stops in front of his office door, a servant opens it for my brother to pass through. I enter the room and go straight to the chair in front of his. I sit and wait for the lecture to begin.

"Now that we're alone, we can be direct with each other, just like we always were..."

"What do you want to know that I haven't already said in front of everyone?" I cut in, somewhat impatient.

"Why? Why won't you renounce this woman?"

"She is the mother of my child," I lean back in the chair, crossing my arms.

"I want you to do a paternity test," Fazza crosses his fingers on the mahogany desk.

"I'll do it, although I find it completely unnecessary. The boy looks just like me, didn't you really notice him?" I ask, incredulous.

"Even so, I want it..."

"Damn it, Fazza!" I run my hand through my hair impatiently.

"Khalil, you're my brother. Even though she is a Sheikha, sister of the emir of Budai, she disappeared for two years. We saw how you went crazy, like a blind snake running in circles. And if she does it again? Wouldn't it be best to cut the problem at the root?"

"And I will," I declare, seeing my brother frown in confusion "I will renounce Elahe in front of everyone, but first, I want her to feel everything I went through, for fleeing, for hiding a child, for living an American life. I want to punish her..."

"Khalil, brother," Fazza huffs, shaking his head "This isn't something you should do. You're clearly angry with her."

"Elahe is mine, and until I decide otherwise, she will remain mine. Now that I have her back, I will keep my eyes on her as much as I can, and when I'm not watching her, there will be eyes on her."

"Brother? Are you sure about this? Are you really decided?"

"Yes, I am," I nod affirmatively.

"And what about our position, what do you want us to do?"

"Accept her. Don't treat her badly, make her feel at home. Elahe won't speak about my treatment of her to her brother. As for you... I don't want any trouble for you with Budai. Not that I'm afraid of Hassan, after all, his sister is married to me. Let's just save this for you," I scratch my beard thoughtfully.

"I had forgotten about Hassan," Fazza huffs "He is quite controlling about family matters; I wouldn't be surprised if we get a visit from him soon."

"I'd be surprised if we don't," I shrug.

"I always suspected he was behind her disappearance," my brother murmurs.

"You suspected? I'm almost certain, but how can you accuse without proof?" I let out a forced laugh.

"Did you ever have a serious conversation with her?"

"No, nothing she says is believable. How can I trust after the craziness she's done? First, she hid the fact that she wasn't pure anymore, then she fled, hid a child. All because, in a moment of anger, I renounced her? With no witnesses? Did she expect me to hear that and find it amusing? To accept her with open arms? I'm a man, flesh and blood, with a huge ego that was shattered at that moment while we were having sex. What more do you want?" I vent, somewhat irritated, as I always do when I think about that day.

"Give her a chance to explain herself; perhaps motherhood has changed her mind..."

"You know better than I do how strong-willed women can be, especially when it comes to us," I huff.

"When it comes to us, it's because we have no patience, and I know you're the same. Sometimes I think it would have been better if you'd stayed with Fernanda."

"Nanda is my friend, nothing more!" I am blunt and direct, hating to have her name brought up as a fiancée.

When I wanted her, no one approved. Now, I won't allow anyone to touch on that subject.

"So is that it? There won't be a divorce?"

"No, not for now," I declare seriously.

"Do you want us to accept her as your wife?" My brother raises his hand, scratching his beard.

"Yes, I do."

"And what about her quarters? Do you want her placed in the wives' wing?" my brother asks, referring to the part of the palace where the wives live. Currently, it is only inhabited by Aiyra, Fazza's mother, and Lâmia, my mother, who rarely stays at the palace, always participating in organizations around the world.

My father's third wife does not live in the palace; she has always chosen to live in another palace.

"I want her in my room. I just need a room for our child..."

"I can place him with the twins; that way, it will be easier for them to feel close," my brother refers to his three-year-old twin children.

"That works for me, but first, I'll discuss it with Elahe."

My brother nods.

"Before you go, sit with me on the sofa so we can talk, relax, and smoke some shisha," Fazza says, rising from his chair.

As eager as I am to see Elahe, I agree.

CHAPTER FIFTEEN

Elahe

"Sheikha?" I lift my eyes as I see the new nanny for Rafiq stopping in front of the door to our room.

My son is sitting on the bed in front of me, playing with some toys we brought with us.

"What's your first name?" I ask, attentive.

"Meira," the woman replies.

"Meira, I want you to inform me of any issues with my son, okay?" I say, being very explicit.

"Yes, ma'am," she nods.

"What will you do with him now?" I ask, looking for an excuse to stay close to my baby.

"I'll take him for a bath..."

"I can do that," I reply, huffing.

The woman looked over her shoulder, making way at the door, soon recognizing my husband entering the room.

"Any problem?" Khalil immediately asks.

"I can take care of our son," I say, rising from the bed where I was lying.

"Rafiq needs to get used to the nanny, hand him over," my husband is direct.

I let out a long sigh as Khalil comes to the bed, picking up the little one in his arms. Rafiq is a calm child, but everything here is new.

"Please, call me if there's any issue," I walk beside Khalil, asking the woman to take my little boy into her arms.

Meira nods.

"She knows what she's doing; she'll take good care of him," Khalil straightens his posture.

I take a step towards my son, giving him a lingering kiss on his cheek.

"Mama..." he smiles with his toothless grin.

I touch his cheek with the tip of my finger, watching as the woman walks away with my baby.

I draw a deep breath, seeing Khalil close the door to the room.

"Where will he sleep?" I ask.

"In the twins' room," Khalil replies, looking around the room.

"I want him close to me!" He looks at me over his shoulder as if I have no reason to speak there.

"He's in this palace; that's what matters. Rest assured, he's being well taken care of."

"Why does he need to be in the twins' room?" I cross my arms.

"They're cousins and almost the same age; it will be good for Rafiq," Khalil turns towards me.

"They must have more than two years' difference; for their age, that's quite a lot!"

Rafiq is just a baby, barely able to walk, let alone be put with three-year-olds.

"No one will mistreat our son..."

"How do you know?"

"Damn it, Elahe! I know, I would never allow anyone to do such a thing to Rafiq!" Khalil begins to walk towards me.

"Given how I was treated, how can you think they won't do the same to our boy? Your brother even asked for a paternity test."

"And I agreed," Khalil starts unbuttoning the first buttons of his shirt while taking slow steps towards me.

"Do you think it's necessary to poke our boy just out of sheer stubbornness?" I raise an eyebrow.

"If it keeps everyone quiet about my paternity, I see no other alternative. I don't want anyone whispering through the walls of this palace that Rafiq isn't my son," Khalil stops walking, standing in front of me.

My eyes focus on his chest, where he clearly shaves because the hair seems still growing. I lift my face, focusing my view on the black beard that defines his features, his pointed, perfect nose.

"No one in this palace will mistreat her; if I hear anything, I want you to let me know," Khalil murmurs in front of me.

"I thought that's what you wanted."

"No one has the right to mistreat her, with just one exception..."

"You," I huff, completing his sentence.

In the face of such anger, I take a step to the side, wanting to distance myself from him, but I don't even have time to take two steps away before he's already grabbing my wrist, pulling me against the wall, pressing his body against mine, while his other hand roughly pulls at my *hijab*, revealing my hair.

"Let's set some survival rules. First, don't turn your back on me, and don't huff in my presence!"

"Asshole," I whisper derisively.

That's enough to make my husband narrow his eyes, raise his hand, and grip my neck.

"Did I hear you right?" he growls.

"I believe so; your hearing shouldn't be bad," I mock in the face of danger.

Khalil may have control over my life, but he doesn't necessarily need control over my habits. I had two years of freedom, two years in which I learned that I don't need to lower myself to anyone.

"Elahe, Elahe," he murmurs as if pronouncing a sentence, tilting his head slightly to the side.

"I hate you for making me live this marriage I don't want! Let me go, let me leave. Why don't you renounce me? I despise you, Khalil!" I spit out the words, my eyes wide in the face of his grip that tightens.

"You want freedom?"

"Yes..." I whisper almost inaudibly.

"Then I'll give it to you, but know that Rafiq will stay with me," he lets a huge mocking smile escape.

"Never!" I use all my strength to struggle against his grip.

Khalil isn't caught off guard; he must have been expecting this reaction from me. Holding both of my hands, bringing them up to the height of my head, he presses his body against mine, his face close to mine, our breaths panting.

"Then the plan remains the same," his mentholated breath clashes with my face, his lips almost brushing against mine "You are mine."

"I hate you!" I feel my eyes shine with anger.

"The feeling is mutual..." our lips touch amidst that frenzy.

The hatred of the moment, our mutual anger.

One person connecting us, the reason for me to stay: our son.

I close my eyes, avoiding looking into those intense black spheres.

I hate to admit Khalil is a handsome man. The only man who made me feel alive, his touches made me want to go further.

Ihab marked me negatively, making me hate the touch of all other men. Khalil marked me in a pleasurable way.

By Allah, why can't I just hate this man? Why do I need to like the effect his hand has on my body?

I can hear him exhaling forcefully as he steps away from me.

"I'm going to take a shower, and after that, we'll have dinner with my family."

He leaves me alone there, tormenting me for needing to be present surrounded by so many people again.

CHAPTER SIXTEEN

Elahe

I descend the last flight of stairs, Khalil walking two steps ahead of me. We are met in the dining room by a long silence, as if I am still the cause of everyone's displeasure.

Khalil pulls out a chair for me to sit in, and does the same for himself, staying by my side.

My eyes soon meet Helena, Fazza's wife. She narrows her eyes at me, as if judging me with just a look.

I raise an eyebrow, refusing to lower my gaze.

Helena might be a very nice woman, but I know she must be hating me at the moment. She has always been very close to Khalil since they married.

Fortunately, soon everyone starts talking. Khalil participates in a conversation with Fazza and his other brother Omar, who is sitting across from us with his wife. I believe there must be more people living in this palace than in my old home in the Zabeel palace.

"Elahe, your brother called me," I turn my face towards the voice of the emir of Agu Dhami.

"What does he want?" Khalil asks.

"He wants to know about his sister, obviously," Fazza shrugs. "Does he not know about your son?"

The man raises an eyebrow.

"*Ah*... No," I murmur, lying.

At the very least, Hassan must not have mentioned Rafiq's name, thus keeping our lie more effective.

"That explains why he didn't ask about the boy."

I almost let out a sigh of relief, but I hold it back.

"What does Hassan want?" Khalil asks again.

"He asked for his sister to visit him," Fazza finally says.

"Then she won't go."

"But... but..." I turn my face towards my husband. "He is my brother, my family."

"You should have thought about that when you ran away. Do you really think I believe the story that Hassan didn't know your whereabouts? He didn't lift a finger to find you. Obviously, he always knew." Khalil looks at me with hatred in his intense black eyes.

"Let me go see them?" I plead in a tone of desperation in front of everyone.

"The answer remains no; you and Rafiq will not leave this palace until I decide otherwise."

"He is my brother!" I emphasize, unafraid of the consequences.

"I don't care that he's your brother! You will stay here, end of story!"

I avert my eyes from his, noticing everyone looking at me, seeing how astonished they are by this brief argument showing possessiveness.

Sheikh Omar's wife, whose name I don't know, looks at me with an *oh* on her lips. Fazza tries to intervene several times, but it's almost impossible.

If Khalil thinks he's going to humiliate me in front of everyone, he's very mistaken. My eyes start to blur with the tears that begin to gather, tears of anger.

In a swift motion, I stand up, pushing the chair back, dragging it across the floor, making those who were silent whisper in unison, *oh*.

Khalil tries to hold my wrist, but I reflexively pull my hand away.

"If you want to humiliate me when we're alone, go ahead. But in front of others, I won't allow it!" I shiver between clenched teeth, breathing heavily.

I clench my hands, turning my back, and before I start walking, I can hear Khalil's chair scraping on the floor.

"Let her go, brother-in-law," Helena says.

I don't look. I see nothing more, just allow myself to leave, wanting as much as possible to be far from all this madness. Perhaps I should thank Helena for intervening, for keeping Khalil away from me. I don't know this place, so I wander through many corridors not knowing where I am, just wanting a calm, private place.

I find a door that leads outside the palace, to its rear. I'm not going to run away; I wouldn't do that without Rafiq, especially since I know I am being watched even from a distance.

I slow my pace, dragging my bare feet over the pebbles, not caring about the dirt, letting silent tears fall from my eyes.

I stop in front of a fountain, crossing my arms, watching the crystal-clear water cascade, the dark night falling over the Emirate, the cool nighttime air, without the intense heat on our skin.

I lose myself in thought, wondering if it was really worth going through everything I have to end up in the hands of my husband, who, contrary to what everyone said about him, is not affectionate or funny at all. It's always the opposite, from the very first moment we were alone.

He never wanted me, he never desired me.

By Allah!

Why won't Khalil give me a divorce? I raise my hand to wipe away the tears falling from my eyes, wondering what I should do.

Knowing that when I'm in his presence he will punish me. Reminding me of the previous day when he laid me on his lap and spanked me so hard that I can still feel it. Who is this Khalil that only I know?

Perhaps I have awakened this in him. The Sheikh's wrath.

I hear footsteps on the floor; I don't turn my face, but I can tell by the scent that it's him. I'm so exhausted that I didn't even bother to check his presence.

"I deeply hope you have a good excuse for this outburst." His voice is present in the open courtyard.

I don't say anything, lowering my face, trying to hold back the tears, wanting to appear strong, at least in front of him.

"Aren't you going to say anything?" he asks again in a whisper.

"I don't want to talk," I murmur with a voice still hoarse from crying.

"Then let's go to our room..."

"I want to be alone," I cut him off.

"That's not an option," Khalil declares.

"I don't want to be punished again today," I whisper weakly.

"I won't do that," At this moment, I raise my eyes, searching his for a hint of sincerity.

Khalil has his head bowed towards me, his eyes half-closed in my direction, his hands in his pockets maintaining his untouchable Sheikh demeanor.

"Promise?" I inquire.

"Yes, now let's go. The nanny reported that Rafiq is crying, asking for his mother."

As soon as he mentioned my son's name, nothing else mattered. I turned, wanting to know where my Rafiq is.

CHAPTER SIXTEEN

Elahe

Rafiq has finally calmed down. I run my hand over his smooth cheek. His breathing is calm, showing that he is sleeping peacefully.

This is all new to him, especially since they insist on keeping me away from him. Out of the corner of my eye, I see Helena enter the children's room. It is a large space, and her children are already asleep.

"Ma'am?" Meire, the nanny, calls me.

"Yes?" I whisper back.

"Take a baby monitor with you, so if we have any issues with the little one, you'll know," she hands me a small device that shows the baby sleeping on its screen. I lift my eyes and see a camera on the bed that displays the feed on the device in the woman's hand.

"Thank you," I say, taking the device.

"Does he usually wake up in the middle of the night?"

"No, it very rarely happens," I reply, leaning over the crib and kissing my little boy's forehead.

His black hair falling over his forehead.

"Please, any untimely sound from him, call me," I ask the woman, who nods.

When I turn my body, Helena is no longer there; she probably just came to check on her children. With one last look at Rafiq, I leave the room, having memorized the path to my bedroom. I feel my stomach growl, knowing I haven't eaten properly, remembering my confrontation with Khalil.

I stop in front of the door to our room, and with a long sigh, I push the door open.

"No, Nanda, it's complicated," I hear Khalil speaking on the phone as soon as I enter the room.

He is sitting on the bed, with the phone to his ear. It seems he is having a conversation with his beloved, and of course, I am jealous, or rather, angry. Because I only receive his worst side. I don't say anything, just ignore him and head straight to the bathroom.

I lock the door, grabbing my phone, and I continue to ignore my brother's messages.

Of course, there are many ultimatums from him, saying that if I don't visit him, Malika will come to see me since he cannot leave the Emirate.

As if it were that easy, if I could, I'd already be there, but my extremely possessive husband thinks it's an outrage.

I don't respond to Hassan, knowing he has information from the Emir of Agu Dhami. I don't want to be the bearer of more bad news.

I stop in front of the bathroom sink, reading Logan's message asking if he can come kidnap me. My friend is simply wonderful, my American brother. I send him a *clown emoji*. And I quickly reply that I am still alive, of course, not mentioning the truth.

I lock my phone again, wash my face, closing my eyes in front of the mirror. I take off my *hijab*, knowing that I am alone in the presence of my husband, whom I don't even know if he is still in the room. I leave the bathroom, holding the baby monitor and my phone in my hand, and place them on a piece of furniture.

Khalil is still sitting on the bed, but this time he is no longer on a call.

What struck me as odd was that the last time I encountered the foreigner, she didn't speak our language. Has she learned it? Probably.

I push that thought aside as I enter the closet, stopping in front of the sleepwear, wanting something discreet. Through the mirror's reflection, I meet my husband's gaze. He is sitting on our bed, his eyes fixed on me.

I stay like this for long seconds, until breaking the gaze, hearing his footsteps dragging across the room, knowing he is coming toward me, the sound getting closer.

"I want to visit my brother!" I say, looking at him through the mirror.

My eyes travel down his outfit: flannel pants, touching his feet, and a thin V-neck jacket. This might be the first time I've seen him not in a suit. I haven't even seen him in a tunic, except for our wedding.

"I thought we already discussed this," he crosses his arms.

"Yes, we discussed it in front of everyone, and you didn't even bother to listen to me," I turn my body to face him.

"And you, as a good protagonist, gave your little performance," he retorts.

"I'm just asking for this. Please?"

He remains silent, raises his hand, rubbing his beard as if he's really considering the matter.

"I can't leave Agu Dhami right now. Fazza is asking for my help with some contracts with the Queen of England. We will have many meetings with the Congress of our Emirate."

I didn't know Khalil was involved in Emirate transactions; apparently, he is more involved in the matter than I imagined.

"Let me go alone with our son."

"You must be crazy," he mocks, letting out a forced laugh.

"No, I'm not. Just give me two days..."

"No, Elahe! I don't trust you."

I slap my hand on my waist, hating all of this.

"I hate you!" I huff. "Why don't you call your beloved again?" Amidst my anger, I show my jealousy.

"Who said she's my beloved?" He tilts his head to the side.

"Are you kidding me?" I scoff.

"I'm not. Fernanda is my friend, that's all..."

"And now I believe in fairy tales," I run my hand over any pajamas, wanting to leave.

But once again I am intercepted. He grabs my wrist, pulling me against his chest, and I fall like a leaf caught in the wind.

"We're talking. What a horrible habit of stamping your feet," he holds my chin, lifting it towards his face.

"Why do you always prefer her?" I murmur in disgust.

"It was just a call."

"Who guarantees me that?" His eyes analyze every part of my face.

"I guarantee you. I don't have another one, I didn't have one, and I won't have one while my contract with you is in force..."

"You treat me like a contract?" I mock.

"Yes, my contract," I huff in the middle of his words. "Are you huffing, wife? I should punish you."

I widen my eyes, not wanting that.

"But I will spare you... for now. Do you want to see your brother? I'll give you the two days, but with one condition."

His hand slides down my back, pressing my body against his.

"And what would that condition be?" I ask, anesthetized.

"You in my bed, with no clothes on while I indulge in your beautiful curves..."

I widen my eyes.

CHAPTER SEVENTEEN

Elahe

Khalil lowers his face to my neck, kissing it, his beard brushing against my skin.

"I'm damnedly in need of sex," he murmurs, grabbing my hair.

"Have you been faithful these two years?" I ask weakly as he lifts his face, amid the kisses.

"I've never gone so long without sex, damn my wife who ran away!" He tightens his grip on my hair, making me gasp.

"Should I believe you?" I murmur.

"Oh, you definitely should," Khalil loosens his grip on my hair, holding my waist, turning my body so that I am facing away from him.

He doesn't wait for my response, he lowers the zipper of my tunic on my back, letting it fall at my feet, then he opens the clasp of my bra, letting it fall to the floor.

His hand moves my hair to the side, returning to kiss my neck, moving to my shoulder, holding again at my waist, turning me to face him. Before I can cover my breast, he grabs my wrists, preventing the act.

"What do you say?"

"Is 'no' not an option?" I ask, holding back a smile.

"No, I don't accept 'no.'"

Before I have a chance to say anything, he picks me up and sits me on his lap, my legs entwined around his body.

"Now tell me the truth?" he asks, his face close to mine.

"About what?"

"Have you stayed faithful?"

"With a small baby, I haven't had many opportunities, especially since out of these two years, I spent nine months with a big belly," our noses touch.

"Not with that man surrounding you?" He narrows his eyes.

"He's my friend, there was never any attraction, it was always just friendship, I... I..." I let the sentence die as Khalil lays me down in the middle of the bed.

"What about you?" he asks, removing his coat with one knee resting on the bed.

I let out a long sigh, looking at his bare chest, knowing he isn't wearing underwear, as his member is erect, almost escaping from the waistband of his pants.

"I... I..." I stutter again. "I have a block with other men, I don't like being touched."

"But I touch you," Khalil furrows his brow.

"Yes, and with you, it has always been different. I think it's because people always spoke well of you, Malika always praising you as the ideal husband. Maybe my subconscious prepared for you, but when another man tried to touch me in Los Angeles, I would withdraw. Even in the bar, I hated it when people wanted to greet me cordially, I don't like it." I shake my head in a negative gesture, as if I hate thinking about it.

"Why is that?" he asks, curious.

"My first time was horrible. I was deceived, humiliated, and completely exposed to all my family."

"Do you want to talk about it?"

"It's not a story I like to recall..." I whisper, lost in that day when I ruined my life for the first time.

"And if I ask you to tell me?"

"I will tell you..."

"Just answer me with a yes or no," I nod my head. "Did that man take advantage of you? Was it without your consent?"

"It was with my consent. I thought that was what I wanted, until I realized something was wrong, that it shouldn't hurt like that. I saw in his eyes that it was a trap. It hurt... it hurt in my soul and physically. Seeing the disappointment in my brother's eyes, but still, he has always been by my side. Hassan wanted to tell you the truth, I stopped him... that's my trauma," I sigh.

Khalil growls, as if cursing himself for something. He doesn't say anything, only lowers his body onto mine, kissing my belly, moving up with his beard causing that delicious tingling.

He pauses at my breast, licking the swollen nipple.

Then he takes it in his mouth, circling with his tongue.

Holding my waist, he moves up to my face, his eyes fixed on mine.

"Damn... why didn't you say this before the wedding?" he asks, murmuring with a hoarse voice.

"I was afraid. Afraid of being rejected, humiliated, used again. And in the end, that's what happened..." My voice trails off.

"I would never stop wanting you because you weren't a virgin anymore. From the first time I saw you hanging on the fence at the stud farm, I wanted you, even though I was a complete egomaniac. Out of all the Arab women, your gaze captivated me the most..."

He recalls our first meeting at my brother's stud farm, where I played with my horse that still lives in the same place.

"I cursed you," I remember telling him.

"I think that made me want you even more, impossible as it may seem to me."

"But there was always the other woman..." I murmur.

"I will always have her as my friend, my sister-in-law's sister. Fernanda never wanted a serious commitment with me; she wasn't born for our culture, and I realized that too late, when I hurt you on our wedding day. When I didn't choose to stay by your side. You are my Elahe, it is my commitment to take care of you, and our child..."

He barely finishes speaking before he's bringing our lips together, a slow, deliberate kiss, exploring every corner of my mouth.

"Damn, but I still want to punish you a lot, for every damned day you made me suffer waiting for you," Khalil bites my lip hard, making me moan into the kiss.

He gets off the bed, removing his pants, revealing his erect member, so hard that it gently touches his stomach.

"But today all we'll do is gentle sex. I need to mark your body with my hands, make you forget any trace of someone else having touched you..."

He lies back on top of me, his member brushing against my entrance, his hand moving under my neck, pressing firmly. He enters my pussy, sliding in.

"Damn, so wet," he growls, joining my lips with his.

The wet kiss mixes with his penis entering my pussy. The back-and-forth movements are deliciously irresistible.

"I won't last long, you're so ready," he murmurs into the kiss. "I've been without sex for so long, it's like I'm coming off a diet, falling into a delicious sea of sweets..."

Khalil smiles with our lips connected.

"Please..." I whisper, begging him not to stop. Loving the delicious sensation it causes.

"Tell me if it hurts because now I'm going to fuck this pussy hard..."

I bite my lip during the kiss as he starts thrusting quickly, intensifying the movements, hard and strong, slamming into my pelvis.

"Khalil..." I call his name in a moan.

"Come for me, Elahe, come..." he growls.

Allowing it to take over me, I let myself be carried away by the wave of pleasure. My husband pumps hard inside me, his hot jets going deep.

"Oh, damn... this is just wonderful!" Khalil lets his body fall on top of mine.

We stay like this for long seconds until he gets off me, lying beside me.

"Our first time should have been like this," he murmurs, closing his eyes.

I watch my husband's features as he lies relaxed in front of me, looking calm, not at all like the man who insists on punishing me.

He opens his eyes.

"Let's bathe to clean up..." he says, reaching out his hand to me.

"Can I go to Budai tomorrow?" I ask, holding his hand.

"Yes, but I'm still not happy about it," I can hear him huffing.

I really want to see my family, but maybe Khalil has opened a door for me, a side of him I hadn't known before.

It was good to have him inside me; I wanted to repeat it. This side of Khalil is a new experience.

CHAPTER NINETEEN

Elahe

Sleep won't come. I keep tossing in bed, feeling uncomfortable.

"*By Allah*! Will you just stay still?" Khalil whispers beside me.

"I can't, I'm wide awake," I huff in frustration. "I think I'm going to check on Rafiq."

I make a move to get out of bed, but my husband stops me by placing his hand over my chest, making me lie down again.

"He's fine, the baby monitor is next to the crib. Look over there; you'll see the little guy is sleeping like a baby."

The fact that my son is sleeping so peacefully on the monitor makes me feel calmer, but at the same time, insecure. Insecure simply because he is so calm. I must be going completely crazy.

"Then I'll do something else; I can't sleep," I try again to raise my body, but Khalil has his arm over me, pinching my nipple through the fabric of my nightgown. "Ouch! Are you out of your mind?"

"You're not going anywhere. I can give you a distraction..."

I'm about to ask what he's talking about when he pulls me onto his body, making me sit on his member.

"What do you think you're doing?" I ask, seeing his eyes shine through the dim light coming through the thin curtain on the balcony window.

"I'm going to give you a pastime..."

"Is it possible that everything can be reduced to this?" I huff, soon feeling his hand gripping my neck.

"You huffed at me, wife?" he growls. I can feel his penis starting to press against me through the fabric of my panties.

Khalil is wearing only underwear; he made me take a bath with him, which was too intimate and completely embarrassing, even though it didn't seem so to him, who, from my perspective, acted naturally. There was nothing in our bath together; it was all to me, I didn't even look at him properly. It's hard to believe that couples share such intimacy.

"Aren't you taking a break?" I ask, even though I want more of this.

"Admit you want it as much as I do," he releases my neck, holding the hem of my nightgown, pulling it up over my head. Leaving me only in my panties.

"Do you always jump to conclusions?" I murmur, letting a smile escape.

"I bet your mouth around my cock, that you're wet, slick, and wishing that I fuck you..."

My eyes widen. What is Khalil thinking?

His hand slides down my waist, I hold onto his firm chest, feeling his member press against my pussy, that mere act makes me desire him.

My husband pulls at my panties, tearing them.

"Khalil!" I exclaim his name in reprimand.

"Oh, just as I imagined," I sigh, feeling his finger on my pussy.

"This... this... It feels so strange," I murmur, beginning to understand how good sex can be, not just good, but wonderful.

"A strange good? Or bad?" His finger circles my clitoris, making me gasp.

"Good... oh... very good..." I let out a moan.

"My sweet wife, enjoying a cock. How right I was, now you're going to suck my dick..." he removes his hand from my pussy.

"No, this... this..." I shake my head in shock.

"Oh, it wouldn't be you if you didn't contradict me. I want your mouth sucking me, Elahe, now," he orders.

With a sudden move, I get off him, Khalil pulls down his underwear, revealing his member, hard, strong in its full glory.

He leans back against the headboard, sitting up partially. He leans forward to grab my hand, pulling me between his legs.

"Now get down, take my cock in your mouth. This isn't strange, just as I've enjoyed your pussy, you can do the same with my cock. We're married, intimacy between us is something you'll need to get used to, at least until I've done everything I want with every curve of yours..."

I lower my face, looking for a few seconds; the light from outside illuminates his member, making the liquid at the tip shine. Who am I trying to fool? I want this...

"Get on all fours, stick your ass up, give me the best view of your body while you take my cock in your mouth..." I do as he says, my face positioned in front of his penis.

I run my tongue over my lips.

I hold his penis in my hand, feeling the veins, the intensity of its thickness. It's slim, but my hand doesn't close completely around it, it's long, my hand moves up and down, feeling it.

"Bring your mouth to it, suck it, don't use your teeth, just suck, use your tongue, get messy..." my husband murmurs, making me raise my eyes toward him.

Without diverting my gaze, I lower my face. Using my mouth, I bring his member to it, sucking as Khalil instructed, using my tongue. Going as far as I can, feeling the salty taste at the tip.

"Ah... that..." he growls, placing his hand on my hair, holding a ponytail. "Move up and down, as if it were your pussy taking me, lick it with your tongue..."

I pull the member from my mouth, without lifting my head, only raising my eyes, and say:

"What do you mean?" I ask, sticking my tongue out, licking the entire length of his penis.

I do it several times, hearing my husband breathing heavily.

"You fucking slut..." he growls as I resume sucking his penis, going as far as I can, sucking with eagerness.

Until I feel him press my head to go deeper, making me gag and want to pull away in my shock.

"No, you're not pulling your mouth off my cock. I want to feel the head of my cock touch your throat, and as a good obedient wife, you're going to suck all of it..."

He barely finishes speaking and pushes my head to go further, I gag again, which makes him smile, a wicked, naughty smile, as if he enjoys it. That's when I realized he likes it, feels more intense pleasure when I go further, I let him dominate, sucking his penis, making my tongue pop from how much I salivate over his member.

"Oh, fuck... I'm going to come and I want you to swallow it all... without shame, just so you see that this is intimacy. You swallowing all my cum!"

He growls as he holds my head, moaning loudly, feeling hot jets in my mouth, making me swallow it all. I didn't even have a chance to gag, I swallowed it all. Khalil pulls me by the hair, making me sit on his lap again. His other hand caresses my cheek.

"I think I have a new addiction," he murmurs, tracing my lip with his finger.

I don't say anything; I'm frightened by how intense he is in bed, always possessive, pulling me, squeezing me. His penis hasn't even reached its normal size and it's already pressing against me again.

"Feel my cock?" he asks.

"On one condition. Let go of my hair; it hurts a lot. Not now, but later it gets sore..."

"Don't you like me holding you tight?" Khalil asks.

"Strangely, I do, but you tend to be very intense. Let me guide you a little..."

"Do you want to dominate me, wife?" He raises an eyebrow.

"Will you let me?"

"Go ahead," Khalil releases my hair, bringing his hands behind his head, giving me the freedom to sit on his member.

I let the penis enter my pussy, sliding in, I start going up and down, holding onto his shoulder. My husband's eyes are on me the entire time.

"Ride my cock," he asks, unable to contain himself.

I do as he says, starting to grind on the penis, going up and down, gyrating, feeling it take me completely.

"Ah..." he murmurs. "I can't keep my hands off you..."

Soon, he grabs my ass, giving it a hard slap.

"Khalil... that's a low blow," I moan, biting my lip.

"A low blow is having a hot wife and her being away from me for two years. Now I want to fuck you everywhere, every moment that's convenient for me... you are entirely mine, Elahe," he growls, squeezing my ass tightly.

I wrap my arms around his neck, gyrating with more intensity, going in and out of his penis, feeling that wave of pleasure taking over me.

Our panting breaths in the room, sweaty bodies, soon leading us to surrender to the moment, with him coming inside me again. I collapse exhausted on top of him, my eyes heavy, fatigue taking over, sleep finally arriving.

"I think I made you exercise now," he declares with a playful voice.

"I'm sleepy," I murmur.

"Lie down, let me clean you up, you can sleep..."

Khalil whispers for the first time in a tender tone with me.

I lie on my side in bed, hearing him go to the bathroom, the sound of water, and soon I fall asleep.

CHAPTER TWENTY

Elahe

I am welcomed to Zabeel's palace with many hugs; I don't even have time to say anything. Malika and Ayda are squeezing me in their arms with Rafiq between us...

"Guys," I say amid my laughter, trying to rein them in but loving all that human warmth.

"Be quiet, let us catch up with you," Malika protests, not letting go.

"You deserve this," Ayda completes Malika's sentence.

My two sisters-in-law seem like two crazies, which makes me burst into a loud laugh.

"You two are scaring Rafiq," I declare, watching them pull away.

Malika has her beautiful green eyes filled with tears, just like Ayda, who is a bit taller than Mali.

My brothers join them, with Hassan stopping next to his wife and Abdul next to Ayda.

"Come live with us, please?" Malika pouts.

"I would love to, but..."

"She's still married. Still..." Hassan says with a lot of certainty in that 'still.'

Coming towards me, he hugs me. Rafiq joins the hug, not quite understanding what is happening.

"Why did you say 'still' with so much certainty?" I ask curiously.

Hassan immediately picks up his nephew, ignoring my question. That's typical of him, pretending he didn't hear.

"You are even more beautiful in person, you know," he says affectionately to his nephew, Rafiq giving a wide, toothless grin. My little guy claps his hands, celebrating.

"He and Hakan will get along great," Abdul makes his presence known, coming towards me and giving me a tight bear hug with his enormous arms.

"I can't wait to see my nephews," I say as Abdul releases the hug.

"Latifa is around with Grandma," Malika replies.

"That's so Maya, carrying her granddaughter everywhere," I tease.

Latifa is my brother's 2-year-old daughter. He always boasted that his first child would be a boy, but a beautiful girl with green eyes like her mother came along. Of course, this only heightened my brother's protective nature. Meanwhile, Abdul and Ayda had a lovely little boy, just two months older than Rafiq.

"Hakan just went to change the diaper with the nanny; he'll be back soon," Ayda responds, talking about their son.

"We need a changing table downstairs; it's a shame for a palace this size to be without one nearby. Ayda is pregnant, she shouldn't have to keep going up and down the stairs when she wants to change the baby's diaper," Malika asserts.

My sisters-in-law have nannies for both their children, but they always texted saying how much they love doing it when they can.

"What do you mean, Ayda is pregnant?" I ask, crossing my arms, feigning offense at not knowing.

"In my defense, I found out a week ago, and they wouldn't let me tell you," Ayda, who is also my cousin on my mother's side, raises her hands in surrender.

"You're all so fake," I stick out my tongue at them, laughing.

Hassan never lets go of my son; he holds him in his arms as if he wants to protect his nephew. We head to the lounge, where there are many toys scattered on the floor. My brother places my son down to sit there. Malika kneels beside Rafiq, playing with him.

"What about you guys?" I ask Hassan. "Aren't you going to try for a boy?"

I tease him about his first unsuccessful attempt.

"Now that the serious parliamentary commitments are over, we decided to have another child, riding the wave with Abdul. That way, we can make the mess together," Hassan laughs.

"Mess? Just wait, it might be another girl," Malika shrugs.

"If it's another girl, we'll try a third time until our Youssef arrives," he has always made it clear that he would name his son after our grandfather, just as Abdul named his son after our father.

"You're all crazy," I shake my head.

"Speaking of crazy..." Hassan crosses his legs, laughing at what he's about to say. "Latifa said this morning that my beard was horrendous. With those words, the girl is a genius; I didn't even mind her cursing my big beard."

Everyone around laughed. Latifa seems to have come out of an encyclopedia; at two years old, she learns everything around her with ease, and obviously, that's another reason for Hassan to be proud of his daughter.

"I blamed her aunt, who stressed me out," Hassan points a finger at me.

"Me?" I widen my eyes. "You liar. Lazy one, blaming me."

"I should record this moment, as it's not every day we see someone call Emir Budai lazy," I lift my face, seeing Maya appear with her granddaughter.

"Maya," I call her name, getting up from the sofa and going over to my brothers' mother.

Latifa, who is walking beside her, runs excitedly towards her mother, curious to see a boy sitting next to Malika. I hug Maya tightly, seeing her as a second mother since I was also raised under her watchful eyes.

"I was so thrilled when Hassan told me you were back. Does Zenda know you're here in Zabeel?"

"If no one has told her, she doesn't know..."

"By Allah! I'll let her know then, because otherwise, I'll be hearing Aunt Zenda complaining later," Ayda quickly gets up from her husband's side.

I let out a laugh, seeing that nothing has changed here. I hold Maya's hand, walking back to the center of the room where I see my son interacting with his cousin. It's incredible how quickly this little one adapts to people, even though he was used to seeing all my family through video calls. I sit next to the back of my brother's armchair, whispering to him:

"What did you mean by 'soon I won't be married anymore'?"

Hassan doesn't look my way, only scratches his beard, mumbling back, making me lower my head to listen.

"I talked to Fazza; we're studying the necessary measures for your divorce without Khalil having to publicly renounce you."

I open my mouth several times, but no words come out.

"Khalil doesn't know about this; for all intents and purposes, I'm handling it alone. Fazza, like me, does not want this union. It has harmed both families. You two have already been harmed enough; we should never have accepted this marriage. Therefore, the best we can do is find a loophole in the contract. In the meantime, you continue to play the role of his wife, just don't run away again. I'll sort it out."

This is the Hassan I know, always wanting to control everything around him; I would have been surprised if he hadn't taken some action.

"Sure..." I whisper back, letting my voice fade amidst my thoughts.

I don't recognize myself; I should be happy about this, it's what I've always wanted from the beginning.

CHAPTER TWENTY-ONE

Elahe

I decided to spend the night with my son. I didn't want to sleep away from him; at least this way, I keep my mind occupied with him, though this proved ineffective in the long run, as Rafiq quickly falls asleep.

I lie on my side, resting my head on my arm, analyzing every feature of my son. His dark hair falling over his forehead, the long black eyelashes inherited from his father, the slight pull of his eyes, much like Khalil's.

How can anyone still doubt that Rafiq is Khalil's child? I picked up my phone several times, but there are no messages from him. How foolish of me! We didn't exchange phone numbers, but he could have called Hassan and asked. Still, he hasn't. What bothers me most is what Hassan said about finding a loophole in our marriage contract.

Khalil doesn't know about this; our family is behind it, orchestrating everything, thinking this is best for both of us. And, in theory, it should be. Khalil hates me, hates every part of me for running away from him, for lying. Perhaps what Hassan is doing is the right choice.

The end, the breakup.

My heart tightens seeing my son caught in this crossfire, such a tiny being having to experience this. In my exhaustion and thoughts, I ended up falling asleep.

"MAMA," MY SON'S VELVETY voice invades my ear.

I smile at the little chubby hand on my cheek. He starts babbling for me to wake up, all wrapped up, calling for mama to wake up. I open my eyes, finding that tangle of messy black hair, a mini replica of his father.

"Hello, my little angel," I whisper with a still-sleepy voice. Rafiq reaches for my hand, standing up, soon stumbling and falling back onto the mattress, playfully spreading his legs as he lies down.

"Me, mama..." my baby asks for his bottle.

I smile at him, getting out of bed. I place my son on the floor and head to the closet to change, so I can go downstairs and have my coffee.

AFTER MY SON HAD HIS bottle, I left him with the children's nanny and headed to the breakfast room.

My mother is there, sitting next to Ayda, whispering in her ear. My steps are heard, causing Zenda to look up at me.

"Ungrateful daughter!" she exclaims, getting up from her chair and walking around the table.

If it were in my childhood days, I'm sure she would have scolded me. Maybe even a few months of punishment. But today, it was different. I received a tight hug from her.

My mother always knew where I was; there was no way to hide it from her, so we preferred to tell her, keeping her informed of everything, making the woman so famous for loving gossip, stay silent.

"How I missed you, ungrateful girl," my mother says in the embrace, her way of showing affection.

I just smile, knowing her well, understanding that this is her way of saying "I love you."

"I missed your lectures," I tease as she holds my hand, studying my face.

"How is your marriage?" As funny as it is, she was the first to ask.

"On cloud nine, we're living in full honeymoon mode," I tease again.

"Elahe Amal! Don't joke about serious matters, because I still have hopes that it all might work out..." It seems Zenda is the only one holding out hope.

"Mother," I sigh, pulling my hand away from hers, "Don't place expectations where there are none."

"We can't think like that..." Mom tries to speak when Hassan interrupts her.

"This union cannot continue. If it were up to me, Elahe wouldn't even leave this palace," his deep voice makes itself heard.

I pull out a chair to sit, my eyes meeting those of my sister-in-law Malika, who has always known me better than anyone, as if we had a connection from the start. I give her a slight shrug, indicating that there's nothing that can be done. Zenda huffs as she walks around the table, looking at me, and speaks again:

"Where is our little Rafiq?"

"In the playroom, with the children's nanny."

My mother said nothing more and went after her grandson.

Tonight, I'll spend another night alone, another day with no news from my husband, as if he doesn't even care about our existence. I begin to eat, lost in my thoughts.

"Fazza called me today," my brother says once the table is almost empty.

"You two have been keeping so many secrets lately," Mali comments, making a funny face at my brother.

"We're trying to arrange this divorce as quickly as possible. Fazza tried to make the brother renounce you, but he didn't accept it, wanting to continue with this madness, causing more harm to both of them. Do you know why he sent you to Budai, sister?"

I turn my face, wanting to know the reason, shaking my head in a negative gesture.

"The Brazilian. It seems she arrived at the Agu Dhami palace yesterday. She came on vacation to visit her sister. According to what Fazza told me, they have nothing, but we know how that reckless boy is..."

"We're talking about my husband Hassan," I hold the napkin in my hand, "not a boy. I know you don't like him. Just as I can't stand him most of the time, but I beg you, never express your hatred in front of Rafiq. After all, Khalil accepted him from the very first time he knew he had a child, without even demanding a paternity test, despite Emir Fazza's request. I want this divorce, I want my freedom in Los Angeles, for Allah! I feel like a fish out of water. I came to soothe my longing for you all, not to speak ill of Khalil. I am as guilty as he is, after all, I am the one who ran away. I love you all with all my heart, and I know you're doing this for my own good, because you love me. But today, just today, I don't want to hear about the Brazilian and Khalil..."

I could feel my eyes welling up with tears, but I quickly held them back, wanting to show strength.

How could Khalil do this? First, he has me in his bed, and then he doesn't give me any news about himself, all because the Brazilian is there?

CHAPTER TWENTY-TWO

Khalil

These meetings that Fazza holds are exhausting. The English have strong opinions when it comes to our Emirate. Fazza always has everything under control; he is astute, constantly proving to everyone that he was born to do this, which isn't the case for me.

I spent the entire morning talking with my brother's parliament when all I wanted was to lie in my bed, seeing my wife's black hair spread across the pillow.

Damn!

She isn't even in the palace. There's no denying it; I can't stop thinking about her. I'm good at ignoring things. I haven't sent her any messages, making it seem like I don't miss her or our son.

Would calling to check on Rafiq imply that I'm only missing him? *Shit!*

She's only been in my life for three days, how can I have this uncontrollable need to have her back? It must be the sex. Not that she's the most experienced woman I've had, but because she's the only one I can have in my bed. Obviously, that's it.

Everything revolves around sex, carnal need. Two years without sex have made me a sex-crazed lunatic now that I have my wife back. I'm still clouded with desire when I walk into the room and find my family gathered, including Fernanda.

She arrived here the day before, right after Elahe left. Having her in our palace always gave me good reasons to laugh, but even she can't lift my mood.

"I see you're still stressed," Nanda comments, looking me in the eye.

I shake my head, letting out my best forced smile as I sit next to my mother.

"I'm upset that I didn't get to see the girl who rose from the ashes," Mom continues on the topic.

"Isn't there a better topic to discuss?" I cross my leg.

"I believe that having a grandchild is the most important topic, especially since I haven't even had the chance to meet him."

"I can't wait to meet little *Khalio*. Helena said he's your mini-me," Fernanda declares with a huge smile on her face.

Nanda learned our language after Helena's persistent urging. She decided to learn since she always came to the Emirate to visit her sister and could never communicate with anyone except me and Fazza.

"She shouldn't have gone on that trip; I haven't even met my grandchild!" I turn my face, seeing a pout on my mother's face as she crosses her arms in indignation.

"There's no need for such drama. They'll both be back tomorrow," I roll my eyes.

"That is if she comes back," I raise my eyes, meeting my brother Fazza's gaze.

"If she doesn't come back, I'll go get her..."

"I don't understand this unyielding need to keep the girl here. Why not let her stay with her family? Just as I want what's best for you, Hassan wants the best for her. This marriage was a mistake; it's clear that you both harm each other. Otherwise, she wouldn't be there now." My brother scratches his beard, raising an eyebrow.

"She's there only to visit her family."

"She shouldn't be in Budai; she should be by your side, finding a place in her schedule to come on a day when you're available."

"Just like Helena went to Brazil without you in our first year of marriage?" I counter my brother's argument.

"My situation is different from yours!" Fazza replies.

"Of course, what I don't understand is why you all insist on involving yourselves in my marriage when I didn't ask for anyone's opinion," I roll my eyes impatiently.

"I've said it before and I'll say it again: we care about you; we want what's best for you," at this moment, Helena turns her face to her husband, making it clear in her look for him to stop mentioning this topic.

"No one in this palace hates her," my sister-in-law starts to speak, "but we all saw how lost you were these two years, not knowing where to turn, completely directionless. Even if you didn't love her at the time, she's your wife, the woman you married."

I didn't say anything; I just listened to what my sister-in-law had to say, reflecting on her words, "*even if at the time you didn't love your wife?*" And who said I love her now? I just want Elahe for my pleasure, for my revenge.

And damn, pleasure is a word that suits her perfectly!

She may be innocent; it's clear on her face that she feels embarrassed every time I ask her to do something more daring. But I want her in my bed. I haven't even done a third of what I plan to do with those beautiful curves, so sweet and delicate, especially when she's not on guard. How did I manage to live two years without her? Without her moans, sighs, and sweaty body riding on top of me.

Damn! She knows how to do it masterfully, and she's just a girl with little experience. I feel like a raving teenager.

"I hope I'm here tomorrow to meet little Rafiq," Nanda says, referring to my son.

"And why wouldn't you be?" I raise an eyebrow.

"I don't know, maybe it's because I arrived and she left?" Fernanda's voice has a skeptical tone.

"Just a coincidence," I shrug.

I admit it wasn't a coincidence. At first, I wasn't going to let Elahe go to Budai, but when Nanda mentioned she was coming to visit her sister, I decided to let her go, thus sparing them a disastrous encounter. But now I'm furious for letting my wife go so far away from me.

I might not have anything with Fernanda anymore, but I once did, and Elahe knows that. Even looking at Nanda doesn't give me the pleasure I once felt. Perhaps our relationship as a couple was never meant to be. She's beautiful, full of life; the man who wins her heart will be very lucky.

But right now, it feels like my world revolves around my runaway wife, the toy I have, and that I could never use.

And now I want to use it, indulge until I'm sick of it.

I SIT ON MY BED AS night falls through the light curtain.

I grab my phone, searching my contacts for Hassan's number, my brother-in-law. I hover over the number until I decide to make the call.

It rings about five times before someone answers.

"Hassan?" I say first, hearing the man take a deep breath on the other end.

"Yes, it's me. What do you want, Khalil?" He is direct.

"I want Elahe's number..."

"You're only now concerned about her?" This time it's me who takes a deep breath.

"Just give me the number," I say, not in the mood for his lectures.

"My sister is busy..." he tries to evade.

"Give me my wife's number!" This time I'm blunt, losing the little patience I have left.

"I don't see why you don't just let Elahe go. If you don't, I will. My sister is too good for you!" he says no more and hangs up.

Damn Sheikh!

It doesn't take long for a message to ping with her number; at least he gave me the contact. I save it in my contacts and immediately call her. I call several times, but it goes straight to voicemail.

Hell!

I send a message to the number with no profile picture, perhaps because she doesn't have my number saved.

I don't send just two or three messages; I send several.

And I get no response.

She stays *online* at various times, but she doesn't even bother to reply. I give up, irritated. Consumed with anger, I send one last message:

"Know that tomorrow your ass will be so red that you'll never dare to ignore one of my messages again!"

CHAPTER TWENTY-THREE

Elahe

Hassan made me late on several occasions, causing me to leave Budai only in the afternoon. The private jet landed at a property far from the main palace of Agu Dhami, sparing me from the paparazzi, which is quite odd. I even wonder if Fazza is paying to hush up my return.

It's impossible that they haven't discovered it yet, or that none of the palace staff has spread the news. Rafiq is asleep on my lap; I stroke his sweaty hair while watching through the car window as we approach the palace.

I let out a long sigh, recalling Khalil's messages and how annoyed he sounded between the lines. I didn't think, I just didn't reply. He didn't say she was back, took a while to get in touch with me—did he think I'd snap my fingers and respond like a good wife?

When I read his last message, my fingers itched to reply, but I didn't, sticking to the original plan, knowing I was literally in hot water. But at least this way he knows that I'm aware of everything. The car slowed down and stopped in front of the palace.

Soon someone opens my door; I look up to see a staff member. Carefully, I exit the car first, then take my son in my arms. Rafiq murmurs something and lays his little head back on my shoulder, still drowsy.

"Do you need any help, madam?" the man offers, and I shake my head.

I walk with Rafiq nestled against my neck, making my way through the grand entrance of the private part of the palace, where only the royal family resides. I remove my shoes at the door, placing one foot over the other.

With my hand on my son's back to keep him from falling, I am accompanied by a staff member who opens the door to the room, announcing my arrival. I regret not mentioning that there was no need to announce me.

I step into the room, finding several pairs of eyes on me when all I'm looking for is him. I find him standing next to a sofa, with his friend sitting beside him.

They seemed to be in a conversation and were quite close.

"Hello everyone," I murmur, hoping they'll resume their conversations.

But that's not what happened, as if they were waiting for some reaction from me. Fortunately, Rafiq decided to wake up at that moment, lifting his little head to me.

"Mama, I woke up..." the baby, with a scrunched face and slightly reddened cheeks, looks at me, still processing his mood.

"I thought I'd have to come and get you," I look up to see Khalil standing beside me.

How did I not see him standing here? When did he get close?

"I'm here now," I huff.

"You're huffing?"—he whispers so low it's almost inaudible.

"Just your impression," I raise an eyebrow, looking down at Rafiq.

My little boy raises his dark eyes toward his father.

"I usually have a good sense of things," he whispers again.

"And I usually notice when I'm left waiting for news and the reason is hidden," I murmur back.

Khalil lets out a side smile, somewhat mocking, irritated.

"Oh, is this our little guy?" I hear a feminine voice beside us.

I immediately recognize Lâmia, Khalil's mother; she hasn't changed a bit in these two years.

"Since your ungrateful father didn't introduce you, I decided to satisfy my curiosity myself," she says, raising her hand to touch his cheek, lowering her voice to continue speaking—"Khalil, this isn't the place to air dirty laundry, the girl just arrived."

With her other hand, I saw Lâmia pinch her son's arm almost imperceptibly. I couldn't help but smile. My son raised his chubby little arms, wanting to be held by his grandmother.

"Oh, dear, it's amazing how alike they are; he's a photocopy of Khalil," the woman says with a radiant gleam in her eyes—"He reminds me of your father when he was just a baby and didn't have a hard head."

She speaks with amusement, asking to hold Rafiq. My son lets out one of his beautiful toothless smiles, showing his few teeth.

"Have I thanked you today for always talking too much?" Khalil huffs at his mother.

Clearly, Khalil has a lot of respect for his mother, as she reprimands him, and he doesn't even do anything, just showing his displeasure on his face.

"The lab will come tomorrow," Fazza announces loudly for everyone to hear.

"Lab for what?" Lâmia asks, with Rafiq in her arms, walking around the room showing objects to her grandson.

"The boy's paternity test," the emir responds.

"They're going to do a paternity test on him?" Lâmia asks, astonished.

"How can we be sure he's the boy's father?" Fazza answers respectfully to his late father's second wife.

"Against evidence, there are no arguments. Look at this boy! Unless you're blind, it's obvious he's Khalil's son. Why subject the boy to a thorough test? What do you think, Elahe?"

I widen my eyes, Khalil still beside me. No one has ever cared to ask my opinion in this palace.

"I've already said it's unnecessary, unless Khalil has some lost brother out there. Even though I've been away from my husband, I've remained faithful to him..."

"And what proof do we have of that?" My eyes met Sheikh Fazza's, who had an arched eyebrow aimed at me.

"Enough, Fazza," I turn my face toward my husband. "How much intrusion into my life? I've made it clear that I know what I'm doing. I agreed to this test only to shut him up, to have plausible proof that he is my son, but my mother is right. There's no need to subject Rafiq to a test when he is my child. At all costs, you want to find some argument. He is my son, just accept that."

"I want what's best for you, just as her family wants what's best for her. You both have caused each other enough harm. Why don't you renounce her now, in front of everyone?" Fazza declares with his authoritative voice, trying to use his persuasive power over his brother.

Khalil lowers his face toward me, his black eyes fixed on mine, as if he's considering it.

"I..." he murmurs, letting the sentence trail off.

At that moment, Rafiq chose to cry. As if he understood what was happening, he called out to me with his little, plaintive voice:

"Mama..."

Without paying attention to anything else, I go to the baby. Lâmia hands him to me, whispering just for me to hear:

"Perhaps he really does feel it. I believe that divorce isn't in your plans..."

"Once again, Fazza, brother, thank you," I heard Khalil declare, irritated with his brother.

I didn't hear anything else as I left the room, not bothering to look back at them. I still don't know what to do in this palace.

CHAPTER TWENTY-FOUR

Elahe

After leaving the room, Lâmia followed me, guiding me to her bedroom where I calmed my son.

"How do I get to my room?" I ask, seeing my phone is dead, knowing that all my things are in Khalil's room.

My mother-in-law gives me directions and asks me to leave Rafiq with her. I look at my little boy, seeing that he is calm, playing with his grandmother, so I decide to leave him.

"I'll be back soon," I murmur.

"Don't worry, dear. I love babies, especially when they are so cute," the woman starts making faces, and I smile, leaving them alone.

Lâmia was the only one in this palace who welcomed me well, who accepted my son.

I know I'm an intruder in this place, but I won't accept Fazza raising his voice again in Rafiq's presence.

I don't know what happened after I left, but I could hear raised voices from Khalil and Fazza.

The brothers have never fought, and knowing that I might be the reason makes everything worse.

I grip the edge of my *hijab*, wrapping it around my finger.

I hear voices approaching, stop walking, recognizing Khalil's voice and the Brazilian woman; she speaks our language.

"You need to stay calm; they only want what's best for you," she says clearly.

"Fazza insists on meddling in my life," I can hear him snorting.

"He's concerned..."

"I'm fed up! It's all so confusing..." he cuts her off.

I stop dead in my tracks, my feet planted on the ground.

"Everything will work out. Just don't end up fighting with your brother. Trust me, he just wants the best for you, Kha," she calls him by a nickname?

Maybe this familiarity gives me a twinge of jealousy.

The two turn the corner, and their eyes meet mine. The woman shows no reaction, maybe a bit of pity.

"What are you doing here, Elahe?" he asks, surprised.

I lift my face as they walk towards me and stop in front of me.

"I'm going to my room," the woman whispers.

"Don't feel pressured by my presence..." I don't finish speaking before I'm already passing by the beautiful Brazilian woman.

Maybe I am an intruder after all.

I leave them behind, quickening my steps, wanting to get out of there, to escape again, to go far away. I want my brief life back.

I turn a corner, forgetting the way to the room. Damn it!

My vision becomes blurry. Tears are threatening to fall. I realize I'm lost in this enormous palace as I enter a dead-end corridor.

"What a big mess!" I murmur to myself.

"Lost?" I hear my husband's voice loudly behind me.

I don't turn around; I keep staring at the wall, with no escape, clenching my hands into fists.

"Why don't you renounce me?" I choose this moment to turn around, bumping into his chest, practically pressed against me.

"Because I don't want to," he shrugs as if I were his property.

My eyes burning, tears of anger. I raise my hand, gripping his white tunic tightly.

"I don't want you," I declare through clenched teeth.

"You're clearing your throat..." Khalil tilts his head to the side.

"No, I'm not! I'm being direct. Give me the divorce. I hate you, Khalil," I push against his chest.

He pulls away, looking down, lifting his eyes toward me, narrowing them. I didn't have time to escape; he was soon holding both of my wrists, pressing me against the wall. His legs squeezing mine, my arms above my head, held by just one of his hands.

"Which part didn't you understand? I'm not giving you a divorce. You are mine!"

At that moment, the tears I had tried so hard to hold back fell, like a cascade. I wanted to struggle, to escape from him. But it was in vain; he is stronger than me.

"I hate you, I hate you so much..." my voice hoarse, tired, exhausted "Let me go, let me be, just let me go..."

My voice fades, I lower my face, avoiding looking at his beautiful masculine features.

"Hey..." His long fingers grip my chin, lifting my face.

"Why don't you give me freedom, when you clearly prefer her?" I whisper, feeling the humiliation on my face again.

"Who said that?" he asks as if I were crazy.

"I'm not foolish! I only serve as a tool of punishment in your hands, a sexual object. Why? Why? Why?" I repeat several times.

Khalil looks at me for a long time before finally saying with a sigh:

"Maybe I was a bit harsh with you."

"A bit? You're being modest," I huff.

"Your irritating habit of huffing in front of me," I can see him gritting his teeth.

"See, everything about me irritates you," I close my eyes.

"That's where you're wrong! Everything about you fascinates me, and I curse myself every day for having rejected you that night. If I had been different, even for a short time, if I hadn't acted out of recklessness, I would have you here. I'd see my son grow in your belly,

I'd whisper Adhan in his ear. Do you think I don't blame myself? You are mine, my Elahe!"

"You would renounce me," I murmur, remembering the incident in the room.

"I don't know if I would have the courage to say it three times, not when I desire you so strongly in my bed, in my arms," Khalil tightens his jaw.

I open my eyes, finding his face lowered, analyzing each of my features.

"Always this..."

"Sex?" he asks, making me nod "If you knew how much I enjoy sex, hard and hot. Especially with a stubborn girl, with a sweet little pussy."

He whispered so low that I almost didn't hear.

"I don't want that, Khalil!" Although my body speaks otherwise, feeling a slight tingling between my legs.

"Shall we go to our room to sort this out?" Khalil presses his body against mine.

"I'm not going to sort anything out with sex!" I resist, hearing him huff.

Maybe Khalil realizes he won't get anything from me at this moment, so he releases my hands, and I hold them together, feeling where it was previously painful.

"Alright. You win, no sex. But this will only increase your punishment for the night..."

"I wouldn't expect anything different from you," I roll my eyes.

My husband takes my hand, intertwining his fingers with mine.

"Let's go to our room; you need to understand a few things."

"As long as it doesn't involve sex," I whisper.

"Ah, my dear wife! Tonight you'll moan so much, you'll forget your name by the end of it," he says with conviction.

"Your self-confidence is enviable," I wipe my eye, catching his attention as he stops walking, placing his hand on my cheek.

"There's nothing I hate more than seeing a woman cry, especially when the reason is me, and she's the mother of my child. I don't want to see you like this anymore," he whispers, holding my face, looking around.

He lowers his face, giving me a long, gentle kiss. His delicate lips caressing mine.

"Don't say things you can't follow through," I whisper with his lips pressed to mine.

"Always on the defensive, you're simply the most resilient woman I've ever met..."

"Maybe you have too strong a personality," I shrug.

He resumes interlacing his fingers with mine, heading towards our room.

CHAPTER TWENTY-FIVE

Elahe

"Has he fallen asleep?" I ask, seeing Khalil lying on the bed while fiddling with his phone.

He lifts his gaze towards me, his head resting on his hand with his elbow on the pillow.

"We were playing, and before I knew it, he was already asleep," he frowns in a funny way.

"He was tired. The trip exhausted him, and your mother made him expend a lot of energy. Lâmia has a way with that," I smile, thinking of my mother-in-law.

"She certainly does," Khalil rolls his eyes.

"Do we need to go downstairs for dinner?" I ask, wanting to avoid another encounter with Khalil's family.

"Yes," he sits up calmly, avoiding waking our son.

"I've already bathed and I'm ready to go down," I declare, despite my displeasure.

Lâmia handed over our son, and Khalil took him while I showered. It's amazing how easily Khalil connects with Rafiq; the two of them have bonded in a fascinating way.

Just then, someone knocks on the door.

"Sir, it's me, Meire," the woman's feminine voice comes from the other side of the door.

"Go put on your hijab, and I'll open the door."

Khalil asks while I head to the closet to pick out a scarf.

I can hear their voices while Khalil gives some instructions. When I return to the room, Meire is taking the baby from his father's arms. She smiles at me, asking for permission as she leaves with my son, my heart aching every time he is taken to sleep in that distant room.

"I don't want Rafiq sleeping away from us anymore," I say, stopping in front of the mirror to check my hijab covering my hair.

I lift my eyes to follow Khalil's steps as he walks towards me, stopping behind my body, watching me through the mirror's reflection.

"I'll ask them to make a room for him closer to ours," I frown at the fact that he just agreed with me.

"Are you sick?" I tease, seeing him crack a half-smile.

"I'm not, I just want Rafiq closer to us too," he shrugs.

"After everything that happened today, I want him close; I don't want others looking at him with hatred. Rafiq is innocent," I lower my gaze, seeing his hand on my waist.

It's so strange to see a man behind me, a man who is my husband, touching me with an intimacy I've never had with anyone else.

He's taller than me, and our contrast looks nice together, with a small step he shortens the distance between us, pressing his body against mine.

"No one will ever harm our child," he declares with conviction.

I turn my body, looking at his white tunic.

"Let's go downstairs," Khalil requests.

"Can you say I'm indisposed?" I lift my face.

"No, because you're coming with me," I huff "Are you huffing again?"

My husband grabs my wrist, guiding me out of the room.

"You can let go of my wrist," I ask, pulling my hand away "I'm not running away! You're making me feel like an animal."

He releases my hand, allowing me to walk beside him.

"Now we look civilized," I murmur sarcastically.

"Civilized isn't what I want to do with you tonight," my husband whispers.

"You're crazy..." I roll my eyes "It seems like you don't even remember what I said today."

"Okay, okay. Can we talk while I give you some affection?"

"Affection?" we talk quietly as we go down the stairs.

"Yes, trust me, you'll like it, it will leave you very relaxed," I lift my face, finding a mischievous smile on his lips.

"I don't know why I still expect something serious from you," I shake my head as we enter the dining room, finding everyone already seated.

"I'm being so serious, you have no idea how much," Khalil says in a normal tone, making me blush in front of his family.

"Of course, I imagine. Your serious side is totally enviable," I murmur, knowing the others heard, seeing Khalil pull out a chair for me to sit.

I sit down, looking distractedly at the Brazilian woman seated in front of me. She's beautiful, her hair covered by the hijab out of respect for her sister, but she doesn't follow our religion, leaving some curly strands visible on the side. Her full lips contrast with her dark skin. How to deal with the fact that she's incredibly beautiful and was once my husband's girlfriend?

Khalil sits beside me, I feel his hand on my thigh, not intentionally, I turn my face towards him and realize he did it as if it were normal. The conversation among the family continues despite our arrival, so I choose to remain silent.

"Elahe?" I lift my eyes to meet Helena's. "Tomorrow we're going to the stables. I remember you said you love horses. How about joining us?"

I open my mouth in a small, almost imperceptible "oh," not expecting the invitation.

"Oh..." I clear my throat. "Sure. That sounds nice."

"We'll go in the morning when the men are at the parliament for most of the day..."

"All this to get away, sister-in-law?" Khalil mocks from my side.

"If Fazza goes, he'll steal the show," Fernanda scoffs from across the table.

"You say that because you think you ride well. Little do you know, she was raised around horses," Fazza casually points at me, drawing attention to me.

"Do you know how to ride, Elahe?" Fernanda asks me for the first time.

"Yes," I frown. "I think I still should."

In these two years, I've been away from my roots, not practicing what I've always loved doing—riding horses—and knowing I'll see horses again makes me a little more motivated.

"Nonsense, it's probably like riding a bike," the woman declares as if we were good friends.

"You should see the pony Fazza bought for Helena after she fell off the horse," Khalil says with a mocking tone.

"Screw you, Khalil! I'd much rather have my little pony that keeps me closer to the ground," I watch Helena stick her tongue out at Khalil.

Their outgoing mood doesn't seem the same as when I arrived. Could this invitation be an attempt to include me in something?

"If you want, I can ask them to bring your horse," I meet Fazza's gaze, wondering about his intention with this approach now.

"Hadi is in a competition. My sister had to take him after her horse got injured. It's good, at least he's still doing what we used to do," I shrug.

Hadi is my horse, but since my disappearance, he started getting sick on his own. So, when my sister's horse got injured, I asked them to use him. Hassan didn't question it, and seeing the photos of them together made me happy.

"What did you do?" Lâmia, who is at the table, asks curiously.

"Show jumping. I took some vaulting classes, but I started falling off the horse a lot, and Hassan thought I might end up with a broken body part. Of course, at the time, he managed to persuade my father to pull me out of the classes."

"Vaulting is that thing where you stand on the horse and do some risky acrobatics, right?" I nod, seeing Lâmia whistle.

"I spent most of my childhood at my family's stables. I think wanting to live away from my mother's watchful eyes helped."

Soon, the topic changed, and I almost thanked them for forgetting I was there. When everyone was distracted in their conversations, Khalil leaned his face close to my ear and said:

"Vaulting, huh? If you want to ride me, I wouldn't mind. I'm a great guinea pig."

I turn my face to find his close to mine.

"You're worthless," I shake my head.

"And who said I was worth anything?" He gives a cheeky smile, squeezing my thigh, which he only released to take a drink.

Having this extroverted side of him is good, funny, even though it's always in a cheeky manner.

CHAPTER TWENTY-SIX

Elahe

I covered my mouth to stifle a yawn. I'm trying to catch my husband's attention, hinting that I'm ready to go to bed. But he's deeply engaged in a heated conversation with his brother.

From what it seems, they're not discussing my marriage, which is a good sign. I turn my face to find Helena's eyes fixed on me, as if she's trying to decipher something. As soon as she notices my gaze, she smiles—not a forced smile, but a relaxed one, as if she finds the situation somewhat amusing.

"My husband," Helena calls Fazza's attention, drawing the attention of both men, who stop talking. "I'm taking Safira and Layla with us to the stables tomorrow."

"Oh..." Her husband is taken aback by the intrusion, but the arched eyebrow of Helena makes it clear that she interrupted because, like me, she wants to get out of there. "Okay, they can go."

Fazza has four daughters from his previous marriages: Safira, Layla, and Jamile are from his first wife, and Aysha is his daughter with the second wife. I don't know much about them; all I know is that Helena maintains a good relationship with the first ex-wife of the Sheikh, and as for the second, she abandoned her baby daughter. Today, Aysha is four years old and considers Helena as a mother.

Khalil, who was looking at Helena, turns his face towards me. I fake a yawn in response to his gaze, covering my mouth with my hand, and he notices.

"We'll talk about this tomorrow," he said in a good tone to his brother. "Do you want to leave?"

He addresses me, and I nod, getting up from the sofa.

"I'll do the same," Lâmia says as she gets up beside me. "I'll check on my grandson to see him sleep a bit more. When you go to the stables tomorrow, leave him with me."

My mother-in-law makes a little pout.

"Oh..." I let slip. "If it won't be a bother."

"Never. Helena always helps me with the NGOs I direct. If you want to know more about them, you can talk to me. They're wonderful organizations that have helped our people a lot."

"I'd definitely love to," I smile at her as I see my husband come to my side.

"Shall we go?" he asks.

I nod, and Lâmia says her goodbyes, heading in another direction while I follow Khalil towards the stairs.

"Did you ask your mother to be nice to me?" I ask suspiciously.

"No, Lâmia sees the good in everyone. It's no wonder she was always the peacemaker wife that mine had. Aiyra was always the impulsive one."

"At least there aren't only impulsive wives in Zabeel," I joke, remembering my own mother.

"You could say that Aiyra and Zenda are on the same level of craziness," he compares Fazza's mother to mine.

I feel my husband's hand on my back. It's strange for him to do this; technically, we're still in public.

"Why did you choose to study abroad?" I ask curiously.

"Because I wanted, for once in my life, to be known as Khalil, not as Sheikh Khalil, son of the Emir of Agu Dhami, brother of the next Emir. At Harvard, I was known as Khalil the Arab; in some cases, some people knew I was a Sheikh. But it didn't affect my friendships. Not to mention the main reason..." I lift my face, meeting a mischievous smile on his lips.

"I bet it's about a woman," I roll my eyes.

"All kinds, without shame, no rules, just one night and nothing more," he says casually.

"At least you can't say you didn't enjoy yourself," I tease.

"I have to agree with that...

"Did you consider leaving our culture and living there? Like an American?"

"If you ask Fazza, he'll say I shouldn't have gone to America. According to him, I'm too Americanized. But it never crossed my mind to live there, to make the United States my home, because here has always been my place. Did I enjoy living there? I did. But it was a part of my life that I needed to experience to be here today. And let's be honest, I can't stand seeing those Americans touching women with such intimacy in public, just like that friend of yours wanted to touch you."

"It's just touches..."

"No, especially when the woman in question is mine. No other man should even dream of touching her because she is mine, solely mine!"

I shake my head as we stop in front of his bedroom door, watching him push the door open. I go in first, letting out a long sigh as I feel Khalil's body behind mine.

"Any more curiosities about me?" he asks, holding the tip of my *hijab*, pulling it off my head.

"What's the craziest thing you've ever done?" I ask.

Khalil unzips the back of my tunic.

"Agreeing to go into that bar. I think it had to happen, as I didn't want to go there at all, Brayden insisted," he says, letting the fabric fall to my feet.

"Brayden, the American who was with you at the bar that day?"

"Yes, that's him."

"So, we weren't supposed to meet?" I turn my body, starting to get used to being naked in front of him.

"In theory, no," he shrugs.

"Are you thinking about giving me a divorce?" I ask, seeing him become thoughtful.

He doesn't say anything, just removes his tunic, leaving him in only white underwear that hugs his defined thighs.

My husband takes my hand, running his hand down my back as he removes my bra.

"Lie face down in the middle of the bed," he whispers, pointing to the center of the bed.

"No punishment?" I ask as he holds the waistband of my panties and pulls them down, sliding his fingers along my thighs.

"Unless you want it..." he raises an eyebrow slightly.

"Oh! No," I quickly lie down on the bed, my entire body shivering.

Khalil lets out a forced smile, moves around, and grabs a bottle from the drawer next to the bed.

He kneels beside me, and I watch him open the small bottle and drop a few drops onto my back.

"What's this?"

"Relaxing oil," he whispers, reaching out and dimming the light above the headboard, lowering the ambient light.

Khalil places a foot on either side of my body. I close my eyes, feeling his hand slide over my back, spreading the oil he's using.

His hands are firm, moving up to my neck, squeezing, making me shiver, then moving down, squeezing my ass. He maintains a slow rhythm, a combination of relaxation and pleasure.

"Turn over..." he murmurs.

And that's what I did, with him still over my feet but giving me space to move, dropping oil on my belly, moving upwards, letting drops fall onto my breasts.

THE SHEIKH'S FORBIDDEN BRIDE 121

"Regarding your question earlier, do you want me to give you a divorce?"

Our eyes lock, my body silently pleading for his.

"I don't think I want to talk about it," I murmur.

"Don't want to because you're unsure?" Khalil slides his hand down my belly, squeezing, moving up to my breasts, squeezing them hard. With his movements, I feel his penis pressing against my pussy.

"Yes, I'm unsure," I whisper.

"Then I'm getting to where I want to be..."

"And what's your goal?" I close my eyes, letting out a sigh.

"Your regret," I open my eyes, Khalil has a wicked smile on his lips.

I don't say anything as his touches become more intense, pinching my nipple, squeezing them hard, moving down to my pussy where he drops more oil. His hand parts my folds, his fingers getting messy in my center.

"Did you like the massage I gave you?" Khalil asks.

"Oh, yes..." I sigh, feeling his finger enter my pussy.

"And now can you tell me if you're relaxed or sexually frustrated?" Khalil asks, pulling his finger out of me, making me grunt in dissatisfaction.

"Grunting, wife? I don't even need your answer; I already know you want my cock, fucking that pussy," I lower my gaze, watching him free his member. "I shouldn't give you pleasure; you pissed me off the night before, you didn't even respond to me. Do you know how angry that made me?"

Khalil starts to change his expression, removes all his underwear, and runs his hand along his penis.

"You didn't tell me she was here either," I retort.

"I've said countless times that she's just a friend!" His voice is irritated.

"Logan is also my friend, so what?" Mentioning my friend wasn't the best idea.

"It's the fucking fact that you have male friends!"

I didn't have time to protest as he was already turning my body, making me get on all fours. Quickly, his cock entered my pussy, forcefully sliding along my lubricated walls. My husband grabbed my hair firmly, pulling it back.

"Khalil... oh..." the pleasure made me gasp. "Please, it hurts..." I plead through the tug on my hair.

"Say you're mine, Elahe," he demands in a deep voice. "Say... say... say..."

With each demand, he thrusts with more intensity, gripping my scalp tightly.

"No one can touch you, no one can desire you, you were born to be mine. You are mine, and I want you to say it now..."

His possessive side took over, dominating me fiercely, making me moan at various moments. His aggressiveness left me speechless, the pain merging with pleasure.

"I'm yours... oh... I'm solely yours... Khalil..." I bite my lips, feeling him slow down, releasing my hair.

"Then sit on my lap and ride my cock, like the good, obedient wife you are..." He sits down, making me position myself on my knees.

I turn towards him. I crawl between his legs, sitting in the middle of them, holding onto his neck, our faces close.

I sit on his cock, reintroducing it into my pussy, sliding up and down. I move in and out, our eyes locked on each other.

"Accept it, Elahe, you are mine..." he whispers, brushing my sweaty hair off my chest and pushing it back.

Our mouths meet in a slow kiss, a gentle melody, as I rise and fall, grinding on his cock. I start to increase the speed as the kiss becomes more heated.

Khalil moans in the kiss, his hand gripping my back. In the midst of this intoxicating rhythm, we give ourselves up. The orgasm hits me with Khalil calling my name loudly. We stay like this for long seconds. My husband helps me off him. We are both exhausted.

"Come, let's bathe," he extends his hand.

I hold his fingers, getting up from the bed, but didn't expect him to grab my ass, wrapping my legs around his waist.

"Do you know how to dance, Elahe?" he asks, his face close to mine.

"What kind of dance?"

"Belly dance?" I frown, not understanding the reason for the question.

"Yes, it's been a while since I danced, but I know how."

We enter the bathroom with him turning on the shower.

"Then I want you to dance for me, in those short costumes. I'm crazy about women dancing, and just thinking about you giving me a private show makes my cock hard. I can't help but smile."

"I'm not sure if I have the courage, it's too bold..." I make a face.

"You know you can do it because you're incredibly delicious, and my body desires you day and night..."

We step under the water with him kissing my lips.

"Khalil..." I murmur his name.

"I'm going to bury myself in these curves just one more time," he whispers, pressing my body against the cold shower wall. "It's so good to fuck this pussy."

CHAPTER TWENTY-SEVEN

Elahe

I'm still apprehensive about going to the horse ranch. Khalil left early with his brothers, not even having breakfast with the family. The thought of being near Fernanda makes me even more nervous, that flutter in my stomach making me think of dreadful things. It's strange because I don't know what it's like to be next to the person who once shared a bed with my husband.

The same man who groans my name, who begs me to be his. Who grips every part of my body. Did he do the same with her?

And what if I'm just another one in his arms?

I know it's different because I'm married to him. But what about physically?

It's all so confusing, a feeling of possession. Am I jealous because he was with other women before me?

I let out a long sigh as I descend the last flight of stairs. I turn my face, encountering Helena and Fazza's two daughters.

"Are you ready?" I find it odd to hear Helena speaking in the plural, turning my face to see Fernanda coming down the stairs behind me.

"I was born ready, sister," the woman coming down right behind me smiles as she speaks.

"Let's hurry," little Layla says.

The women nodded, heading towards the house's exit.

THE DRIVE TO THE RANCH was filled with Layla and Safira asking a million questions. Helena answered most of them. It's amazing how Helena has the answers at the tip of her tongue for each one, as if she was born to do this. The car stops in front of the ranch, the first to get out were the girls. I get out, looking around. The place is large, with two open areas for the horses to train, and the red sand where they trot.

"I love this place," Helena says, stopping next to me.

"It really is beautiful," I whisper amidst my thoughts.

Layla was the first to run towards the covered ranch. The girl has her beautiful black hair flying, indicating that she hasn't yet become a young woman, unlike her sister who already wears the *hijab*.

We continue walking into the covered area, where Layla is already at the fence watching the horses train.

"I wish I had brought my training clothes," Safira pouts.

"We can't stay long, girls. You know how your father hates us lingering here..."

"Daddy is a pain sometimes," Safira crosses her arms.

"I agree with that," I whisper in a loud thought.

Everyone looks at me, surprised, when Fernanda bursts into loud laughter.

"See? I'm not the only one who thinks so," the woman declares, holding back her tears of laughter.

"Wow, the way you paint my husband..." Helena makes a face.

"Sister, you love him, it's different. From the outside, we see how he thinks he owns the world..."

"Which is almost true. The only luck is that he only rules one Emirate," I complete Fernanda's sentence, not realizing I was taking her side.

We were interrupted by the girls asking to see the stalls and the other horses. We agreed as they went ahead.

My phone starts ringing. I take it out of the pocket of my tunic, seeing my friend's image on a video call.

"Do you mind if I take this call from my friend?" I ask as we walk.

"Friend?" Helena asks, surprised.

"Don't pay her any mind, answer," Fernanda, who is walking among us, didn't even care.

"I would refuse, but it's always so hard to get in touch with him because of the time difference."

They agreed again, and I accept Logan's video call. He soon appears with his tousled blonde hair, tattooed chest, and unshaven beard.

"Wow, Logan! Did some animal run over you?"

"Hey, sweetheart," he says with a hoarse, sleepy voice.

"Did you just wake up?" It's strange for him to call me at this hour.

"Just wanted to let someone know to set off fireworks because the old man died," he scratches his head.

Despite his stubbornness, I know he's feeling it deep down.

"I need to close the bar, I'm forced to go to that shit," Logan says as he gets up, walking around his apartment.

"Sorry, Logh..." I murmur.

"Don't be sorry, kitten, he was already working overtime here," my friend shrugs, placing his phone on a counter as he walks through his kitchen. "Where are you? Bolotinha isn't around, right?"

"He's not here. I'm at the ranch with two, *uh*...," I struggle to find the right words, scrunching up my nose as I continue, "friends."

I tilt the phone slightly to the side, showing Fernanda and Helena.

"Girls, this is my friend Logan," I declare, "Logan, these are Fernanda and Helena."

"With all due respect, Khalil has good reasons to be jealous of you," Fernanda replies, eyeing my friend with desire.

"*Argh*," Logan shakes his head, "The possessiveness of that man disgusts me."

"You're the one who's too available," I tease Logan.

"I'm not available, I just give myself to sad women," he mocks, and I notice Logan's eyes constantly drifting to look at Fernanda.

"Definitely."

"I need to hang up, Lenny is calling me. We should have decided if having a sister was something we wanted," he says, rolling his eyes. Lenny is Logan's older half-sister, and she's always on his tail, asking him to come back to England.

We end the call, and I put my phone away.

"Khalil said you had a friend, he just forgot to mention that he's very good-looking," Fernanda says right away.

"And a total bastard, every night with a different woman," I reply, kicking a small stone.

"If I were Khalil, I'd be jealous," Helena mocks her brother-in-law.

"He's very strange," I shake my head, thinking about my husband.

"Strange how?" Helena asks, curious.

"Strange like, 'say I'm yours,'" I scrunch my nose, watching the two of them burst into laughter.

"That's not strange, sister-in-law, he's just being cautious..."

"And he's afraid of losing you," Fernanda responds as if we weren't talking about the man she's been with before.

"Do you really not care? You've had an affair with him," I turn my face toward Fernanda.

"Yes, we did, and it's in the past. We weren't meant to be together. I'm a woman who likes to show off my body, I love a short bikini, and with Khalil, I'd be stuck in fabric. Even if I loved him, I wouldn't agree to that. I want a man who likes to show off the hot woman I am," she lets out a depraved smile.

"So you never loved him?"

"Love is a strong feeling. My first boyfriend, I loved him, we were together for almost ten years, and he decided to trade it all for a moment, betraying me. That's why I don't give my heart to anyone else."

I remain silent, not knowing what to say, when Fernanda speaks again:

"I know it's complicated, if I were you, I'd hate the bitch who had been with my husband," she laughs, "But know that since the moment you got married, nothing has happened between us, and nothing ever will. Khalil is just my friend. A good friend. And if you want, I can stay away if that helps you two get along. Khalil can be incredibly stubborn. He doesn't tell me what happens between you two, but I know he's somewhat possessive and is probably intimidating you. But deep down, he's a good man. He just hasn't realized yet that he loves you, which is evident in the way he looks at you."

I open my mouth several times, unable to hate Fernanda; she's just an innocent in this whole messed-up marriage.

"Don't end your friendship because of me. I think love is far from being something acceptable in this marriage," I let out a sad laugh.

"I think if you give it a chance, you'll see it could work out..." Helena responds.

"I think we've hurt each other too much for it to work out," I shrug.

I tell the two women about what happened to make me run away from him, my journey over the past two years, my friendship with Logan, and they listen attentively as we walk through the bays.

"So you own a bar?" Fernanda asks, still amazed. "Khalil told me, but I thought he was lying."

"Yes, I do. Logan was taking care of it, but now he needs to go to his father's wake. I think we'll have to keep it closed."

"Oh no. Please, let me take care of it? Until your friend comes back, my dream is to visit Los Angeles..."

"Fernanda, please don't make things up," Helena warns her sister.

"I'm serious. I used to work in a bar when I was a teenager. It probably hasn't changed much. I just got fired from my old job, I don't have anything lined up, please, Elahe, I promise to be a good employee."

"You'll need to work, Fernanda. You're not going there for vacation," Helena scolds her sister again.

"Quiet, Helena!" Fernanda puts her hand over her sister's mouth, making me laugh at the scene.

"It's fine with me," I shrug. "I can ask Logan to leave the bar key with Maggie, and if you want, you can stay in my apartment. It's already furnished, and you can *tour* around."

I'm caught off guard by the enthusiastic Brazilian hug. I couldn't help but laugh at her gesture, knowing at that moment that it's impossible to hate this woman, and that literally, she no longer feels anything for my husband.

"Now no one will hold you back," Helena mocks.

"I'm going to send you *tons* of photos, sister."

Layla and Safira chose that moment to catch our attention. Helena went over to see what they were showing.

I stayed behind, watching their contagious joy. My phone vibrates in my pocket, I pull it out and see a message from Khalil. I open it, loading the image he sent, and I can't hide my smile as I see the photo. Rafiq and his father sitting on the lawn, I can see a white lion walking in the background, knowing they must be in Fazza's private area, where he keeps his two wild animals. Khalil, wearing sunglasses, is smiling for the photo while our son does the same.

I stared at the image for a long time, until I decided to set it as my phone's wallpaper. My heart tightens, and I wish I were with them at that moment, wanting to see the two men smiling and playing in person.

CHAPTER TWENTY-EIGHT

Elahe

I focus my attention on my son playing in the middle of the room with his cousins, Zayn, Mohammed, Jamile, and Aysha. Rafiq is the youngest among them; the twins are identical copies of each other, making their Arab features more pronounced than their Brazilian mother's.

The male voices become noticeable, revealing Fazza, Omar, and Khalil walking in right behind them. Fazza sits in his armchair, winking at his wife, while Omar circles the sofa and sits next to his wife. Omar is the older brother of Fazza and Khalil; he usually doesn't talk much, and he and his wife live in the same palace, always remaining discreet.

There is an empty spot next to me, but Khalil does not sit there. Going over to the children, he sits on the floor next to Zayn. Rafiq, who had been distracted with Mohammed, sees his father nearby, gets up with his chubby little legs, and moves close to his father. Khalil extends his arms to the little one, picking him up and leaning back, making it seem like Rafiq had thrown himself with force. Our son bursts into laughter, echoing in the room.

"You're going to break me this way," Khalil plays it up.

Of course, everyone's attention is on them. It's something I have to admit: Khalil has a way with children.

Rafiq, who was on top of his father, makes room for the two boys to join them, leaving all three boys on Khalil, who pretends to be overwhelmed. His white suit is getting dirty from Zayn's hand, which is covered in some sticky substance.

"By Allah, this is getting out of control," Khalil turns carefully, sitting down.

"That's what you get for not having had a childhood," Fazza mocks his brother.

"At least I'm the best uncle," Khalil teases the other brothers present.

"Get out of here, Khalil! I'm the best aunt. Let them grow up, and we'll see if they don't come to Brazil with me," Fernanda chimes in.

"I'll pay to see that," Khalil stands up, brushing off his white suit.

He looks around, soon seeing me and moving to my side where he sits.

"Keep doubting, and we'll see if your son doesn't come along," the woman shrugs as if that's actually possible.

"Now you're really dreaming too big," Khalil leans back in his chair, crossing his legs.

"Changing the subject," Helena chimes in, "Before this topic brings up another Sheikh who is also against this."

She looks at her husband, who is scratching his beard, somewhat annoyed because he hates Fernanda's far-fetched ideas.

"Nanda will be leaving soon," Helena makes a pout.

"That took me by surprise," Fazza declares somewhat astonished.

"I'm going to spend a few days in Los Angeles, believe it or not!" Fernanda finishes with a wide smile on her face.

"What are you going to do in Los Angeles?" Khalil asks curiously.

"Oh, can I say?" She looks at me, and I shrug, not caring about what she's going to say. "Today at the ranch, Elahe's friend called..."

"That American is still keeping in touch with you?" Khalil interrupts Fernanda, turning his irritated gaze toward me.

"He has never stopped keeping in touch..." I shake my head in confusion.

"Stop meddling, Khalil!" Fernanda says, her voice a bit louder. "He called her, and with all due respect, the man is a total hottie. I'd be jealous in your place too, Khalil."

Fernanda mocks Khalil, causing him to give her one of his killer looks.

"Who said I'm jealous?"

"Oh Khalil, you're such a fool!" she shakes her head. "Now, back to the topic... before the jealous one cuts me off again" Khalil growls at her, making me smile at Fernanda's provocation "The handsome friend needs to travel, and I'll be taking care of Elahe's bar. She said I could stay in her apartment."

"You know you're going there to work, not to visit, right?" Fazza interjects.

"I know, little brother-in-law. But the bar is right on the beach, and Ella said her apartment is close by. I can stay at the bar, meet lots of hot Americans, and still work. Not that this will help me with my law career," she shrugs.

"Ella?" Khalil notices she called me by my nickname.

"Yes, Ella said I could call her that."

"By Allah! Helena, I'm going to kill you. Fernanda is going to lead Elahe down the wrong path," Khalil looks angrily at Helena, who arranged our meeting at the ranch.

"You're the Neanderthal," Nanda retorts. "Tell me, Elahe, are there many guys in swim trunks over there?"

"Americans aren't used to wearing swim trunks. Once, I met a Brazilian tourist who said Brazilians are into that, right? But Americans usually wear shorts above the knee. But yes, there are quite a few, especially during the season. Some older ladies go to the bar just to watch the men coming in."

"See? I don't need to convert anything, Khalil. Your wife is smarter than me. How proud!" Nanda receives an angry look from Khalil.

"You're going to sell, donate, give away, or do anything with that dump. I never want you stepping foot in that place again." Khalil turns his irritated face in my direction.

The playful man from before has given way to the possessive one now.

"The bar isn't even in my name," I raise an eyebrow at him.

"So whose name is it in?"

"Logan's. Everything I own is in his name," I answer his question.

"I need to get rid of your phone!"

"Do that, and I'll smash yours into a million pieces," I whisper back.

When I realized it, he was already grabbing my arm tightly.

"Brother!" I hear Fazza's voice calling from afar.

Immediately, Khalil lets go. He lets out a snarl, muttering some word I didn't understand. In a swift movement, he gets up from the sofa and leaves the room, leaving everyone's pitying gazes directed at me.

"Sorry, I didn't mean to make him angry at you," Fernanda declares.

"It's okay, maybe I should have listened to what my brother said."

I get up, picking up my son from the middle of the room. My eyes burning with tears of anger.

I leave, taking my phone out of the pocket of my robe and calling Hassan, asking him to start the divorce paperwork, reminding him that he had made it clear he had found a loophole, a way to make the divorce happen without Khalil needing to disown me.

CHAPTER TWENTY-NINE

Khalil

I didn't show up for dinner, and I don't even know where Elahe is. Night falls, reminding me that I've been here for too long.

Damn! It wasn't supposed to end like this. I let out a long sigh, running my hand over the steering wheel. On my phone, there are several missed messages from my brother; I only sent a quick reply saying I'm fine. I start the car, knowing I need to return to the palace. I shouldn't have lost control there, with everyone watching, with her terrified look.

When it comes to Elahe, I lose control, and knowing she spent two years away, other men touching what should only be touched by me...

Fuck! We're married; she's mine, legally and everything.

I soon enter the palace, heading to the garage, parking the car there. I get out of the car, feeling a bit calmer, knowing that what I did was wrong, but knowing that I won't apologize. I'm a damn hypocrite for knowing she has a friend while I also have a friend. *But fuck!*

My blood boils every time I think that someone else might touch her, a man who isn't me. Who am I kidding? The jealousy is eating me up inside, like a hot ember, burning me. Elahe is mine; everything about her fascinates me, her moans, her sighs, the way she calls my name. The mother of my child, *for Allah*, how her smile is genuine every time our child is involved. My child, blood of my blood, how could I live away from that little boy? As if the air I breathe depended on him, *on them*.

I enter through the back door, crossing a few hallways, finding the room completely dark. I check my watch, realizing that I spent a lot of time reflecting in the car. When I realized I was in no position to demand anything from her, I left, took the first car from the garage, and drove aimlessly until I stopped on a distant street, seeing the massive buildings of Agu Dhami, the small empire my brother runs. Now here I am, walking through the palace corridors, heading toward my room.

"Brother?" I hear Fazza's voice calling as I pass his office.

I take a few steps into his office.

"Do you need something?" I ask.

"I have a document for you to sign," he looks up from some papers. "Could you do it here? It's quick; I just need your signature."

I frown, puzzled by his urgency. We signed many contracts at the parliament this afternoon; I assumed it was another one of those. I approach, taking the pen from his hand without even bothering to look at what it was about, my mind still racing, unable to focus on anything.

"Are you feeling better?" I ask as I hand the pen back to him.

"I think so..." he murmurs, pulling up a chair, sitting across from me. "How did you know Helena was the right woman for you?"

"Do you want to know how I realized I loved Helena? Only her, enough to leave my other wives and be with just her?"

"Yes," I nod my head.

"I realized it when I almost lost her, and more importantly, when there was no room for any other woman in my thoughts, except for her. I thought of her sweet features, from the start of my day to the end of my night. That's when I realized I loved her, and that if I didn't change my way of thinking, I would lose her. And *for Allah*, if that happened, I think I would chase after her to another planet. I changed my ways, changed everything for her. Helena is mine, solely and exclusively mine, but I don't make her feel captive; they like to have their own space. You need to trust her; if she loves you, she won't do anything to disappoint you."

I thought for a while. Fazza's eyes studying my features.

"Even when the marriage started off wrong? Even with her being away for two years?"

"Your case is different from mine, brother. I can't tell you what to do, but if you love her, you need to give her that trust. Elahe comes from a respectable family, and if she says she hasn't been with any other man in those two years, you should trust her."

"She lied about her virginity," I run my hand through my hair, even more confused.

"Do you love her, Khalil?"

"Honestly? I have no idea. What I feel for her, I've never felt for any other woman, this possessive feeling, this inability to bear the thought of another man touching her, not even with Fernanda was it like this. It's like my blood is boiling. I even thought it might be due to the marriage contract," I snort irritably.

"Honestly, I think you should talk to her before it's too late, before you lose her again," he lets the sentence hang.

"I'll never let that happen," I get up from the chair, somewhat irritated.

"Don't think you're in an advantageous position, Khalil. If you love her, make her realize that, make her feel loved, because once you gain a woman's disdain, there's nothing that will make her change her mind."

"What are you talking about?" I ask, raising an eyebrow.

"I just want you to open your eyes," Fazza with his mysterious phrases. "I want the best for you. If you love her, we'll all accept her, just as we are now. If you decide she isn't the right woman, we'll stand by you. Know that regardless of anything, we want the best for you."

I snort at the mystery, leaving his office, heading to my room, wanting to find her, wanting to talk to her, to hear from her sweet mouth, which is mine, knowing that this doesn't fix our problems.

I push the door aside, entering the dimly lit room, seeing her silhouette lying on our bed, but Elahe isn't alone; Rafiq is with her. I stop at the foot of the bed, looking at the two people who make my world turn peacefully. Fazza's words echoing in my mind, you will lose her if you don't change.

I let out a long sigh, clenching my fists, knowing that I don't want to lose either of them, knowing I'd go to hell if necessary, but Elahe will not leave my side.

She is mine!

I decide to take a shower, to wash away the impurities of my day.

CHAPTER THIRTY

Elahe

My eyes are heavy before they open, flashes of last night coming to my mind: Khalil disappearing, my son falling asleep with me, as I sought strength in him, to avoid crying, to avoid falling apart. Hassan sent the divorce contract to Fazza, and he made it clear that he would have Khalil sign without realizing what it was about.

I open my eyes, focusing on Rafiq, who is sleeping peacefully. His breathing is calm. But what grabs my attention is the man lying next to us. When did he show up here?

Our son rests between us while Khalil sleeps peacefully. Rafiq moves his little arms, abruptly opening his eyes; his way of waking up makes me envious, as I'm still processing while my son is already sitting up on the bed.

"Mama" he spots me, throwing himself into my lap. "Yay..."

He declares, ecstatic about sleeping in the same bed as me. Clearly, he doesn't like sleeping in that room away from me. Khalil stirred beside us, a movement that catches the little one's attention, who immediately turns, showing one of his toothless smiles.

"Papa..." Rafiq lets out one of his squeals.

Rafiq hadn't called him "Papa" until yesterday, after he spent most of the morning with his father. Lâmia said that Khalil left to rest between meetings and stayed with Rafiq; that was during the photo he sent me. He probably taught his son to call him that. I admit I melt hearing Rafiq call him that. The little guy throws himself against his father's chest, hugging him.

"Wow," what a greeting—Khalil is caught off guard by the hug.

Rafiq places his hand on Khalil's chest, standing up and starting to bounce on the bed. Without much steadiness on his feet, he soon falls clumsily.

"I wish I could wake up with that energy," Khalil sits on the bed, taking his son into his lap.

"Airplane" Rafiq asks, raising his little arms.

"How? Like this?" He lifts Rafiq, making the airplane motion around the room, the little one laughing.

I sit on the bed; Khalil is wearing a thin V-neck jacket, and as he raises his arm, it shows the mark of his underwear. Their play is interrupted when someone knocks on the door; it's Meire the nanny, and with much difficulty, Rafiq goes with her. He likes the nanny, but what is a nanny compared to Khalil's paternal image?

Finally, we're alone; I'm still sitting on the bed. When he turns towards me. He says nothing, just looks at me for long seconds until finally declaring:

"I was wrong yesterday," he murmurs.

"Wrong?" I ask, raising an eyebrow.

"I shouldn't have treated you that way in front of my family; I know it must have been humiliating.

"As if you knew what that word means," I huff, getting up from the bed, completely ignoring his presence.

"I'm talking to you; can you stop and give me attention?" I inquire, but I continue ignoring him. I go into the closet, seeing him follow me through the mirror's reflection.

"Where were you yesterday?" I cross my arms, turning my body to face him.

"I needed to clear my head..."

"How nice! You needed to clear your head; will it always be like this? Losing control and disappearing? I'm not an object, Khalil, I'm not like a stone; I have feelings, I have emotions!"

I unload everything at once.

"I'm here precisely for that; I don't want to put you through this anymore. I'm sorry because I know I wronged you at that moment..."

"Only at that moment, during the pressure?" I interrupt, asking another question on top of it.

"Yes, only at that moment..."

His sentence dies off, as if making it clear that he wouldn't apologize for any other acts. I've realized this is him; Khalil is possessive, and nothing will change that. He will always interfere in my life, always wanting to make it clear that he's in charge, that he will choose my friendships.

"What are you thinking about?" he asks.

"I'm thinking if you'd like me to forbid you from seeing Fernanda? After all, she's a woman, you're a man, quite different from my relationship with Logan. You had an affair; you slept together, shared your intimacies. Logan is just my friend. "Friend!" And you still have all this possessiveness. I won't stop talking to Logan, not because you want me to. I'm grateful to him; he was there for me when I thought I would fall apart. So, you can destroy my phone, do whatever you want; you'll only get one thing from me: anger!"

I vent, saying everything that was bottled up inside me. If I didn't speak up, he would think he always had control over everything, which is not how it should be.

"I was willing to be the ideal wife, I was ready to open up to you, but I realized that the one thing I wanted not to be interfered with was interfered with. My friendship with Logan."

"So you'd rather choose him over me?" Khalil grits his teeth.

"This isn't about choices! You're my husband, the man who knows all my vulnerabilities behind closed doors, the man who could have been my confidant, but that gap never existed. Logan is my friend, like a brother; our love is brotherly, there was never anything carnal between us. When I told you I had a block regarding men, he was involved in that block, but you chose to ignore it, chose to let your jealousy speak louder. You're the only man I've managed to fully surrender to, as if we were made for each other. But that's fairy tale stuff! Love doesn't exist. Maybe this marriage should never have existed."

Khalil makes a move to step towards me, but I block him.

"Don't touch me, Khalil!" I request firmly.

"You're upset, I know, it will pass," he says with conviction in his voice.

"Do you still think we can make it work?" I ask.

"As long as you're mine, this marriage will always be right..."

"Don't you think about denying me?"

"No, that's the last thing on my mind. You are mine!" He makes that clear.

I wonder if he has already signed the contract, if I'm just a few steps away from my freedom. My heart tightens in my chest. I know this is what I always wanted, but now in practice, it feels different.

My eyes start to blur. The hurt overtakes me, as he once again treats me like an object.

"If that's all, I want to be alone..." I ask.

"Elahe, it breaks my heart to see you like this," he takes another step towards me.

"You should have thought about that before hurting me. Just leave me, Khalil."

I say with a firm voice, every word decided, knowing that this marriage is hurting us both, knowing that it's best for us to separate, even if it's done the wrong way.

"I can't leave you," he whispers.

"Then just give me a few minutes of privacy."

My husband lets out a long sigh, turning his back. After a few steps, he turns back towards me.

"I'm sorry for hurting you, sorry for everything I put you through, any humiliation, that's not me. That's fear, the fear of losing you again. The fear of waking up and not having you beside me sleeping. And if to have you by my side I need to accept your conditions, I will, even your friend" I open my mouth, not expecting this reaction from him.

Khalil said no more, just left the closet. I was left alone, reflective, still firm in my decision, I want the divorce. Maybe this is my only chance to leave this marriage.

CHAPTER THIRTY-ONE

Khalil

Nothing went as expected; I couldn't be honest with her, I didn't express my true feelings. I feel that despite speaking the truth, it wasn't enough. It was weak, not convincing. When I left the bathroom, dressed in my white suit, she was no longer there; she must have gone down for breakfast already. Elahe is upset with me; nothing I said today made her less unyielding.

I was the fool, thinking she was naive. This woman is everything but gullible. And I hurt her with all my dominance, I didn't give her a chance to speak. Anger always taking over me, combined with the fear of losing her. Perhaps the coercion and oppression were the easiest ways I found to keep her with me; scaring her was the quickest escape. But in the midst of this, I didn't count on her strength, her astuteness in always confronting me.

With a long sigh, I leave my room, heading to the breakfast room, my hand in my pocket, thinking of millions of ways to regain her trust. To make her see that this isn't my true essence.

I arrive in the room, looking around, searching for my wife, but she's not there.

"Where is Elahe?" That's the first thing I ask.

"She..." Helena begins to say, with a long sigh.

I narrow my eyes upon realizing that Fazza isn't there either.

"Helena, where is Elahe?" I ask, my voice wavering. "Come on, speak up!"

Something inside me screams, making me shiver.

"Helena!" I call my sister-in-law's name again, knowing she knows where Elahe is.

"She's in Fazza's office, signing the divorce papers..."

"What are you talking about?" I widen my eyes.

"You signed, Khalil. You signed the contract without knowing what it was about..."

I don't let her finish speaking, damn Fazza for deceiving me!

I'm going to smash my brother's face. How could I trust him?

I start running, wanting to stop her from signing the damn contract, I race up the stairs two steps at a time, my breath ragged, as if my heart could come out of my mouth at any moment. Without thinking, I burst into the office, pushing the door open forcefully, it slamming against the wall with a bang.

Elahe is standing by my brother's desk, while I see him next to his fax machine, realizing that the damage is already done.

"No, no, no" I start shaking my head, not believing what I'm seeing.

"Brother, it's done..." Fazza murmurs with his typical look of regret.

"You bastard! How dare you act behind my back? I trusted you!" I grit my teeth as I walk towards them.

"We did this for your own good; it's obvious that you're hurting each other with this doomed marriage..."

"Of course, because you're the damn owner of reason!" I roar amidst my words.

My eyes focus on her, the woman I was thinking just minutes ago of ways to win back. How foolish I was!

"Why?" I shake my head, looking at her.

"I asked you, I asked you to deny me, and you didn't. In return, you always humiliated me, even knowing my torments. We started off wrong; this marriage should never have existed," she fidgets with the edge of her *hijab*.

"You don't get to decide that; you had no right to make this decision without my consent..."

"See? Always wanting to control everything. I decided! I decided for myself, for Rafiq, for everyone around us."

"Our child isn't leaving this palace!" I say what comes to my mind.

"Yes, he is leaving. Rafiq is coming with me..."

"No! No one is taking my child away from me again," I declare resolutely.

"Khalil, he's going with her. When you signed, you renounced your child, letting her take him with her," Fazza says, and it takes me long seconds to process what he has said.

"No, don't tell me you did that..." I turn my face towards my brother.

"I'm sorry, this was the best alternative we found. You'll be able to see your son frequently..."

A forced laugh escapes my throat, unable to believe the amount of nonsense I'm hearing.

"Khalil, I'm not leaving the Emirates. I'll stay in Budai," Elahe declares, drawing my attention.

I slowly turn my face, my vision blurring, my hands clenched into fists, unable to believe what they have done.

"You had no right," it felt like they had opened a hole in my feet and I was falling into freefall.

I didn't want to blink, knowing that if I did, a damn tear would fall.

Damn!

If there were ever a way to feel what it's like to be stabbed in the back, this is definitely it. I turn my face towards my brother.

"I deeply hope, Fazza, that no one ever takes your children from you, because what you did to me, I wouldn't wish even on my worst enemy. HE'S MY SON, DAMN IT, MY SON!"

I raise my voice, catching them off guard.

"He'll still be yours," Elahe says.

"Away from me?" A forced laugh escapes from the depths of my throat, the tear I had been holding back now falls, one after the other.

Damn! I never thought I would be crying, crying out of anger, out of hurt, knowing that I lost her. Seeing her slip through my fingers and not being able to do anything. The situation spiraled out of control.

"Khalil, soon you'll understand that we did this for your own good..." Fazza insists again.

"If you wanted something for my good, you would have prevented her from signing that damn contract. Even after I told you last night that I thought I loved her, that I was confused, you went ahead... went ahead with this damn plan to stab me in the back!"

I turn my back, heading towards the door, my breath quickening, my eyes still blurry.

"Get out of this office, Fazza, leave me alone with her," I grip the doorknob. "If you have any shred of empathy left, give me some privacy."

I see them exchange glances and she nods to him. My brother walks around his desk, heading towards the door.

"Be careful with what you're going to do..."

"Go to hell!" I murmur back, closing the door and locking it.

Elahe

I SWALLOW HARD AS I see Khalil walking towards me. I know he feels deceived, and that was to be expected. But seeing him crying, crying amid his desperation, was beyond what I anticipated.

"You got what you always wanted, didn't you?" he murmurs with a tense voice.

"I always said I would," I whisper back.

He stops in front of me, and I have to lift my head to look him in the eyes.

"And I underestimated you," he allows a small, side smile to appear on his lips.

"We will always be connected in some way, after all, we have a child," I flinch when he tightens his grip around my waist, pulling me to his chest.

"And what about us? What about us, damn it!?" He clenches his jaw tightly.

"When both of us are hurting, it's not a relationship..."

"And if I say that even though I'm no longer your wife, I won't give up on having you by my side?"

I close my eyes, wishing it were easier. But it isn't; it feels like a punishment. How can I stay away from his touch when, at this moment, I'm craving exactly that contact of his hand on my body?

"Khalil..." I murmur his name.

"Open your eyes, Elahe," he asks, and I obey, finding his face close to mine. "Tell me why you took this step, tell me you don't want me by your side? Tell me this goodbye hurts you as much as it hurts me?"

I get lost in the darkness of his eyes, clinging to that vastness.

"It hurts, Khalil, it hurts because I don't want this. But it's necessary, necessary for both of us to heal. There have been many lies; a definitive end is needed for us to have a new beginning."

"What are you trying to say?" His hand moves up to my face, caressing my cheek.

I tilt my head to the side, feeling his hand.

"I'm saying that there's always a new opportunity, but at this moment, it doesn't exist. Let me go, let me miss you, let me long for your touch from a distance. Maybe that way, we'll both appreciate each other's presence more."

Khalil says nothing, his other hand tightening around my waist.

"Stay, Elahe, don't go, let me take care of you, protect you... don't go..." he continues to insist.

"No, I'm going, Khalil," I declare firmly.

"Have I lost you?"

"No, my heart will always belong to the one man who managed to touch my soul..." I am sincere.

"*By Allah!* You're going, but before you go, I need you to promise me that you'll still be mine, even from afar. I need to hear it from your lips, many times, until I'm convinced you'll return..."

"I am yours, Khalil, accept this as time for us to reflect. You might discover that this marriage isn't what you want after all."

"That will never happen. If in two years I've never given myself to anyone, I won't now. For me, this would never exist."

His hand pulls at my *hijab*, my long hair falling over my shoulder.

"My... my... my..." he murmurs with his eyes still stained with tears. "I'll do everything possible to have you by my side again."

I focus on every movement of his until he lowers his face, our lips meeting in a kiss, fervent and wet. His tongue explores every corner of my mouth. We surrender to that moment, as if words were unnecessary. My hand moves up his neck, feeling his skin as Khalil grips the back of my neck.

"Please, stay, Elahe," he asks through the kiss. "Don't leave me."

I feel his tears return, wetting his face, the kiss becoming salty and painful with the goodbye.

"I'm going, Khalil. Now that I've signed the divorce papers, I'm going through with it. I won't stay just to soothe your wounded pride. If we're meant to be together, we'll certainly meet again..." he doesn't let go of my hair, sucking on my lip forcefully.

"Just know that you're going, and you'll take my heart with you. Please, go, but come back to me," we separate from the kiss amid that painful farewell.

Knowing that I'm now, finally, a divorced woman, doesn't bring me relief. On the contrary, it's too painful. Why did Khalil wait until he lost me to take action? Why didn't he win me over from the beginning? The pain of the farewell hurts, but it's necessary.

CHAPTER THIRTY-TWO

Elahe

ONE MONTH LATER...

"Didn't you say he wouldn't be back for another ten days?" Fernanda's muffled voice echoed from the other end of the line.

"Yes, sorry, I meant to tell you he had postponed his return. Did something happen?" I sat on the living room sofa with the phone to my ear.

"Something happened, Ella, something *huge*," she said dramatically "If I tell you, you'll laugh at me."

"Oh, now tell me, I'm curious," I bite my lip, trying to suppress my laughter.

"You know I have some fun at the bar when it's closed, you're aware of that. Well, at least I don't hide it from you, obviously. And if I tell you I was receiving some attention from a tourist—when I say attention, I mean my breasts were out, okay?—and then the bar's door opens, of course, I told the person to leave because it was closed, and guess what? It was him, Logan. Your friend caught me in the act. And he thought he had the right to mock me. But that *badboy* is so arrogant."

I couldn't help it and ended up laughing out loud.

"Sorry, Nanda, but I couldn't hold back. Logan got a taste of his own medicine; I've caught him with women at the bar many times. Looks like the tables have turned on him..."

"ELLA!" Fernanda yells my nickname from the other end of the line. "You mean he does the same thing? The jerk, he said he doesn't do any of that."

"Well, I guess I said too much. You two are really crazy, seriously," I shake my head.

"I'm a good kind of crazy," Nanda mocks from the other end of the line. "Do you know if he's here to stay?"

"I don't know yet, but you can stay in my apartment for as long as you like."

"Thanks, spending these days here has made me feel rejuvenated. I needed this time for myself, away from everything, away from my chaotic routine. I don't think I've had such a good vacation, even in my best dreams," she lets out a laugh.

"If you want, I can check with Logan about his plans..."

"No need to cause more trouble for you. I'll handle it myself. I'll sort things out with Mr. Funny," Nanda mocks, as if she disapproves of Logan's behavior.

I don't blame her, as Logan loves to make fun of everything around him, especially since he comes from a long list of tragedies.

"Patience, a virtue that not all of us have," I tease.

"Look, I have plenty of patience, especially when it comes to your *badboy* friend," I bet she's wrinkling her nose at this moment.

After a few more minutes of conversation, we end the call. If someone had told me I'd become friends with my ex-husband's ex-girlfriend, I'd have thought it was nonsense. Even though I divorced Khalil, I didn't stop Fernanda from going to Los Angeles to stay in my apartment and take care of the bar as she wanted.

I don't plan to return to Santa Monica for now. Not now, with baby Rafiq, making him miss his father's presence.

My friend said he'd be away for forty days, and knowing the bar was in good hands, I made it clear he could stay as long as needed. Nanda messages me almost every day, updating me on her day, sending some photos of the elderly patrons at the bar, even Maggie, Rafiq's former nanny, has become her friend. I think it's impossible not to be affected by this woman's energy.

Except for Logan, but my friend is a case apart, as he loves to mock everyone. I lift my gaze as Malika enters the room, my sister-in-law holding hands with her daughter, who has green eyes. Latifa and Rafiq are only a few months apart in age.

"There you are," my sister-in-law smiles.

Latifa lets go of her mother's hand and goes to the center of the room where her cousin is playing with building blocks.

"Are you going to Agu Dhami tomorrow?" she asks.

"Yes, we are. Khalil can't come here," I shrug.

"I hope Hassan doesn't want to come along," Mali rolls her eyes.

"These men, they have a serious problem thinking they need to interfere in everything," I huff, watching Rafiq hand a toy to his cousin.

"Honestly, Ella, I don't like that he's always meddling in your and Rafiq's well-being..."

"But we're talking about Hassan," I roll my eyes as she smiles. "Although I really don't mind, my brother has always been by my side, holding my hand, making sure nothing falls apart beside me."

"But you miss him, don't you?"

"Yes, the pain of missing him is painful. But I don't know if he could love me, love me after everything we've done to each other. It was only a few days, but they were the most intense days of my life. I think being husband and wife weighed heavily," I let out a long sigh.

"I was always against this divorce. I always knew your destiny was to end up together. And if it's meant to be, it will be..." Malika gives me one of her sincere smiles.

I remain silent, reflective. It's been thirty days since our divorce. At first, he sent messages every day, but they became scarce and eventually stopped altogether. I don't blame him, as I didn't respond to any of them. Except for those about Rafiq, so he wouldn't be left without news about his son.

Fifteen days ago, he came to the Zabeel palace to see our son. He stayed only an afternoon, bringing some gifts that Lâmia sent for the grandson. He didn't even look my way. Maybe he's giving me the time I asked for, or he's truly moved on.

There hasn't been any news about him in the media, except for my appearance and the divorce with Khalil. This subject made headlines in several newspapers, especially since we have a child. It was a long period of paparazzi speculation surrounding our palace, but fortunately, they didn't manage to get any pictures of Rafiq, only knowing of his existence.

And now I need to go to Agu Dhami with Rafiq. It's been fifteen days since Khalil's last visit, and he sent a brief message asking if I could go to Agu Dhami. A brief message, requesting if I could bring our son to him since he can't leave the palace and his mother misses her grandson.

Just thinking about seeing him tomorrow, my heart feels tight in my chest, that same pain, longing, emotion—a mix of feelings making me sweat cold.

CHAPTER THIRTY-THREE

Elahe

I arrived at the Agu Dhami palace and found it oddly quiet. Rafiq is in my lap, playing with the string of my *hijab*.

"Sheikha, please follow me," one of Fazza's servants appears. "The royal family is at the back of the palace."

I nod and follow the man in front of me. It feels strange to be here after a month away, even stranger to know that I am no longer part of this family, and even stranger to know that I am not here as Sheikh Khalil's wife.

We walk down the corridor, and I see the women of the family lined up, looking out at the courtyard. I furrow my brows, not understanding what they are looking at.

As I approach, the first to look at me is Lâmia, who, as always, gives me one of her warm smiles.

"Hello, dear," she turns her body to come towards me.

"Hello, what's going on?" I furrow my brow.

"Oh, it's a man thing. I swear this species should be studied. Fazza and Khalil made a bet on who could make a faster lap around the back of the palace. They used to do this when they were kids, and Fazza kept rubbing it in Khalil's face that he was still winning. And here we are, waiting to see which of the two bearded men will arrive first," Lâmia shakes her head in mockery.

We approach the other women, who all greet me as if I belong here, quite different from the first time I was here. They almost seem to want me here now.

Could Khalil have a hand in this? Though I highly doubt it, considering he's been ignoring me every day.

Lâmia soon takes the baby in her arms. Rafiq seems to like his grandmother, as if they've always known each other.

"Fazza is such a fool," Helena lovingly curses her husband. "How slow they are!"

"Who has the bigger bet?" I ask, stopping next to Helena.

"Uncle Khalil will easily win against Daddy," Safira, Fazza's daughter, looks at me over her shoulder.

"Don't let your father hear that," Helena scolds the girl with a smile, knowing the child is right.

"Why such conviction?" I ask the two of them.

"After you left, Uncle Khalil has been spending most of his time doing some physical exercise. If he's not running, he's at the gym," Safira shrugs, looking ahead anxiously for the two men who haven't appeared yet.

"He misses you, Ella," Helena murmurs beside me.

"It doesn't seem that way," I reply to the woman.

Our conversation is interrupted when one of the men appears first. Khalil comes into view from the side of the garage, wearing a white tank top, his arms sweaty from the physical activity, his hair wet. He runs backward, his back to us, while his brother, Fazza, comes up right behind him. Fazza, the loser, has a smile on his lips.

"I think you need to improve your physical conditioning, brother. The night exercises aren't showing results," Khalil declares loudly, making those who understand the subject know exactly what he's talking about.

"I won't give a fitting response because we have an audience," Fazza, sweating, goes to his wife, who holds out a towel for him.

"*Papa...*" Rafiq recognizes his father and jumps from his grandmother's lap, wanting to go to him.

Khalil turns to find his son. I am captivated by the scene of him bending down to pick up the little boy, even though he's sweaty. It's the perfect image, father and son right there.

His eyes lift, as if searching for someone, until they land on me. He looks at me for long seconds, making something inside me stir — the pain of longing, the desire to go to him and feel his warmth, but we are nothing more now.

My train of thought is broken when Helena makes a joke with her husband, causing me to turn my face toward them, who are beside me.

"That bastard was running while laughing at my face," Fazza says quietly to his wife, and since I was next to them, I heard.

"It was obvious he would win. He's becoming a gym rat," Helena laughs at her husband's expense.

"Daddy, try again next time and you'll make it," Jamile, Fazza's five-year-old daughter, declares with such conviction.

"You think so, Mimi?" I turn my face to see Khalil approaching with Rafiq in his arms.

"My daddy is very good," the little girl crosses her arms, pouting.

"He has a good army of fans, brother," Khalil teases.

Jamile huffs and leaves, stamping her little feet.

"Do you think I'm weak?" Fazza jokes.

"Come to Grandma, your father stinks," Lâmia appears, taking Rafiq from his father's arms.

The woman, being a doting grandmother, immediately starts entertaining the grandson. Fazza, still by his wife's side, endures her laughter at his sweaty and smelly state.

"I know the kind of sweat you like," I widen my eyes upon hearing what Fazza whispers to her.

It's strange to see this side of the Emir of Agu Dhami. I turn my face away, embarrassed, meeting Khalil's eyes. Apparently, he also heard, but unlike me, he doesn't seem to care at all.

I am left speechless in front of Khalil, a month without seeing him, a month of vague messages over the phone.

The lack of action between us is palpable. The tension in the air is almost tangible. He runs his hand through his hair, making me follow his gesture. I blink a few times, coming out of my trance, swallowing hard.

"Here, brother-in-law," Helena throws a towel to him.

"Thanks," he replies, taking the white cloth.

I take a step back as I realize he will pass by me, completely ignoring my presence, as if I were just another person in the palace.

I take a deep breath as he passes by. The smell of sweat is anything but horrible. I must be going crazy, literally crazy. I asked for this time apart, and now he's giving it, but in the process, he's ignoring me.

"Don't take his actions *literally*," Helena says beside me, perhaps noticing my discomfort.

"I thought you were against my relationship with him," I murmur, not understanding.

"We were never against it, Elahe. We just wanted what was best for both of you. And now, seeing you both separated, we realize we were wrong. Instead of insisting on your marriage, we went for the quickest decision. If it were up to this entire family, getting back together would be the right choice. Although we know Khalil can be quite stubborn. But my brother will come after you again, knowing him as I do," Fazza concludes, draping the towel around his neck.

"But what about you?" I murmur, remembering that Khalil was quite upset with his brother.

"We're brothers. It's been a long journey, but I'm still in the process of forgiving him," Fazza gives a forced smile.

We are soon interrupted as we enter the palace.

CHAPTER THIRTY-FOUR

Khalil

I buttoned the last button of my shirt. I ran my hand through my damp hair and saw through my bedroom window that night was falling. I let out a long sigh, losing myself in the sight of my bed, neatly made with pristine white sheets, imagining her lying there, her hair spread out on the pillow, my son bouncing on my lap that morning we woke up together, the damned morning I was betrayed.

I've never begged so much for anyone's presence as I did for hers, but Elahe chose to go away. Every morning I wake up and don't see her by my side is a different pain in my chest. Something that tears me apart. Being away from her for two years wasn't as hard as being away for this one month; it's as if my mind had marked every part of her body, every sigh, every cell of my ex-wife's perfect body. Yes, ex-wife, I am a divorced man.

But now it's different; I know where she is, I know I have a son, a perfect bond with her. Today, when I saw her, something tightened in my chest, an overwhelming desire to pull her to my chest, hug her, take her to a room, and lose myself in her sweet lips. But none of that happened.

Elahe is no longer mine, and she decided it that way. Not that I am the best personification of a man.

Damn it, but being snubbed like this was painful! Knowing that all this crap was plotted behind my back made my ego hurt, even though at the time I begged, and I would still beg a million times.

But this time I'll do things differently; I need some initiative from her, at least a sign that she wants it as much as I do. I picked up my phone from the side table, put it in my pocket, and left the room. I walked down the hallway with my head down, lost in my thoughts, wanting to be with my son. I descended the last flight of stairs into the living room, where I found my family gathered. Rafiq was sitting next to Elahe, so I went over to them, sitting beside my son. He soon recognized me and came to my lap.

I held him under his chubby little arms, letting his bare feet rest on the white of my jeans.

"Daddy..." his childish voice made me smile.

"Hey there, little guy!" I gently pinched his side, making him laugh from the tickling "Wow, on your next visit, I feel like you'll have grown another half a meter..."

I let out a laugh at my exaggeration. Rafiq, brushing his little hand on my face, damn how I miss him being here every day, seeing him grow, the little kid antics he's starting to do.

And all of this because I was denied the right to see my son, even though Elahe stayed in Arabia, he's far away.

Fazza had no right to do that; my brother should have spoken to me first, but no, he thought he was doing what was best for both. Being away from Elahe wasn't in my plans. I held Rafiq on my lap for long minutes until the nanny came to take him and dinner was announced. I heard Elahe making some demands about our son, I focused on her sweet tone, until I realized that the room was practically empty and the nanny was leaving with our son.

I placed my hand on my knee, getting up from the sofa, leaving Elahe behind without even looking in her direction.

"Khalil?" I stopped walking, hearing her wavering voice.

I clenched my fists, turning my body and letting out a long sigh.

I hoped she'd say something; I saw Elahe was nervous, as she swallowed hard, her hands rubbing together.

"Do you want to say something?" I asked, placing my hand in my pants pocket.

I admit that I'm being a damned son of a bitch acting this way with her, when all I want is to pull her into my arms, give her a good spanking, and fuck her so hard that she forgets her name and never sees herself away from me again.

Ah, Elahe, if you knew how much I desire you, you wouldn't look at me with those fearful eyes.

"I... I..." she hesitated twice before speaking all at once "I need to talk to you, alone."

I narrow my eyes; I know that if I'm alone with her, I won't be responsible for my actions, and by Allah, how I want to be alone with her.

But I decide to play hard to get, just to see what her reaction will be.

"I think not; we're no longer married, and it's not appropriate for a woman to be alone with a man with whom she has no familial bond" I raised an eyebrow, seeing her mouth drop open at my unexpected act.

"Are you serious?" She widened her eyes slightly.

"I don't joke around when I'm with someone I'm not close to" this time, I went too far.

Elahe let out a long breath, sighing during the process.

Ah, how I hate that she does that, I hate that she sighs in front of me. I tighten my jaw, wanting at all costs to punish her for sighing in my face. *What the hell, intimacy!*

"Are you really talking about intimacy? What more intimacy than what we've already had?" The woman made a gesture with her hand from me to her.

"I'm talking about the present time; I'm a single man, and well, you are too. What's stopping us from being alone" I finished speaking, seeing her roll her eyes.

"You're a big jerk, go away, I have nothing more to say to you."

Elahe sat back down on the sofa, closing her eyes and taking a deep breath. I may be a big jerk, but I know she's not well.

I walked towards her, seeing that she had opened her eyes, noticing that her naturally rosy cheeks had turned pale.

"Is everything okay, Elahe?" I asked, wondering if I should call for help.

"I'm f..." and she didn't have time to finish, vomiting on my feet.

"Ah..." I was startled to see the woman sick in front of me.

CHAPTER THIRTY-FIVE

Elahe

"Where is her room?" I hear Khalil ask as people continue to enter the room, increasing my embarrassment even more.

"In the east wing," Helena responds.

"Why so far?" Khalil clearly huffs.

I hold my head with my hands, keeping it down, not understanding the cause of this sudden nausea.

The worst part is having vomited at his feet and Khalil not even stepping away from me, staying right by my side.

"Come, I'll take you out of here" he says again, and just as I am about to get up, Khalil bends down and picks me up into his arms.

I close my eyes tightly in embarrassment, holding onto his white shirt.

"Helena, come with me..." I don't know what's happening, but Khalil lets his sentence trail off, letting out a long sigh "Mom?"

"Yes, of course I will," Lamia quickly responds.

"You don't need to hold your breath, unless my smell is bothering you" Khalil murmurs as he walks up the stairs.

It was only then that I realized I had been holding my breath, breathing softly, letting his wonderful scent fill my mind, reminding me of his delicious aroma that I missed. But soon, I chastised myself as he ignored me, snubbing me, making it clear he no longer wants to talk to me.

"Where are you going, son?"

THE SHEIKH'S FORBIDDEN BRIDE

"To my room; I'm not going to walk all the way to the east wing. What if she gets sick again? I still don't understand why you put her so far away..."

"I thought you wanted to keep your distance from each other" Lamia doesn't even let him finish.

Now my doubts were cleared, as I had asked myself the same question when they directed me to that room.

"Mrs. Lamia?" I hear a man's voice call out to my ex-mother-in-law "There's an extremely important call for you."

"But does it have to be now?" the woman questions.

"Go, Mom" Khalil huffs.

The woman doesn't even blink.

Soon I heard the sound of the door being pushed open, and I could smell Khalil's scent pervading the room.

"I wouldn't be surprised if there was no call" Khalil sighed "How are you feeling?"

I open my eyes, still feeling embarrassed.

"I think I'm good enough to stand on the floor" I murmur.

"Yes, but first you're going to take a shower" he walks with me to his bathroom. His walk is calm, as if I were as light as a feather.

He carefully sets me down on the floor, and I wait for him to leave the room, but he doesn't.

"Aren't you going to leave?" I ask, raising my face to look at him.

"Should I?" His voice is soft, with a husky tone.

"Yes, you should..."

Ignoring any possibility of leaving the room, he raised his hand and removed my *hijab*.

"Khalil, I thought we shouldn't be close to each other" I whisper as if my legs were glued to the ground.

"And we shouldn't be" his finger traces down my cheek "But I can't leave you alone, what if you get sick?"

"I bet I won't..."

"Who's to guarantee that?"

Holding onto my shoulder, Khalil made me turn my back to him, moving my hair to the side. He unzipped my tunic, sliding the sleeves down my arms.

I let out a long sigh; this is so wrong, but I want him. The tingling from his touch leaves me in ecstasy.

"Khalil..." I call his name in a plea.

Turning my body, he walks to the shower, turns it on, holds my hand, gently pulling me into the stall, where I step under the stream of water, letting the running water cascade over my body. Completely immersed in the moment.

Knowing his eyes are observing every movement of mine. I run my hand through my hair, the water obscuring my vision, knowing how much I want him there with me.

I turn my face to the side, seeing my ex-husband acting on impulse, I reach out my hand, pulling his hand. Khalil doesn't resist, taking two steps toward me, I take a step forward, pressing my body against his, me naked and wet, him fully clothed and soaked.

"I... I ... — I begin to speak, wanting him to touch me, but he doesn't, staying only in front of me — I hate you, Khalil.

I finally said what had been stuck inside me, my eyes filling with tears, tears of bitterness. The man says nothing, keeping his head down, his eyes analyzing my movements.

"I hate you so much, I hate you for ruining all men in my eyes, I hate you for making me desire you so much, I hate you for being the first thought of my days and the last before I sleep, I hate you for being possessive and yet so protective, and I hate you even more for wanting your hands on my body all the time, as if you had marked me..." I close my eyes, tears burning my face "I should hate you with all my strength, for everything, for these two years, for the way you treated me, but it only made me want you even more... damn... It's so hard to accept that I love you."

THE SHEIKH'S FORBIDDEN BRIDE 165

I open my eyes. Khalil is still standing there, not even saying a word, as if lost in his thoughts. I let out a forced laugh, humiliation taking over me again, showing my vulnerability and being snubbed.

"Get out of this bathroom" I ask, turning my body to face away from him.

The water starts falling on me again as I position myself underneath it. I lower my head, swallowing a sob, knowing I made another mistake.

"Oh, Elahe, if you only knew how much I want you in my arms, you wouldn't have that sad look on your face" I am caught off guard when he positions himself behind me "But don't forget, we are no longer husband and wife."

He whispered in my ear, biting my earlobe.

"I know" I murmur.

"All because you wanted this, I should spank your ass so hard you forget the damn day you made me a divorced man. Remember, Elahe, even if you don't want it, your body will always belong to me, your little cunt will always crave my cock" his hand moves down my waist, heading toward my intimate area as he whispers in my ear.

His eager fingers soon mold my cunt, making me moan, entering my cunt, caressing my folds.

"Do you want an orgasm?" he whispers, pressing his body even closer to mine, his clothes becoming extremely wet.

"Yes... please..." I plead in desperation.

"Well, I won't give that to you" Khalil makes me face him, his wet white shirt revealing his defined chest "Want pleasure? Do you want me, Elahe?"

His voice is broken, I can feel his member pressing against my belly, his hand moves down my back, gripping my buttocks tightly.

"Answer me, Elahe?" He asks again.

"Yes Khalil, I want you" I quickly respond with the answer that was on the tip of my tongue.

"Then be mine, be my wife again, be only mine, this time in the right way, me, you, and our little Rafiq" His other wandering hand moves up my face, caressing my cheek, outlining my lip "Let me make you the happiest woman. I believe a month has been enough time for us to think about a future alone. *Damn*, I miss you every morning when I wake up, every night when I go to sleep, those two years away from you weren't as painful as this month, knowing where you were, knowing that you both belong by my side. Be mine, Elahe, make me yours, let me punish you, oh... how I love to spank you and then fuck you until we're exhausted. Why waste more time when we've already wasted enough? The moment isn't ideal, the circumstances aren't the most favorable, but will you accept being my wife again?"

Tears fall down my face, mixing with the shower water. I never thought I would hear this from him.

"Oh... yes... a thousand times yes!" I wrap my arms around his neck, pulling him into a hug, turning my face away, refusing to kiss him knowing my breath must be terrible.

CHAPTER THIRTY-SIX

Elahe

I put on the robe Khalil handed me.

"I'll have someone bring you some clothes," he declares, undoing the first buttons of his wet shirt.

I blink a few times, as if hypnotized by his fingers unbuttoning his shirt. In my daze, I stumble out of the bathroom, tripping over my own feet. I heard him let out a laugh as I left the bathroom. I looked around the room, still the same as the last time I was here.

"Your phone is ringing" I turn my body to see Khalil walking toward me, also wearing a robe.

I pick up my phone, seeing Logan's name on the screen. I lift my face, waiting for some reaction from him upon seeing my friend's name, but he gave no sign.

Or rather, he tried not to.

"Aren't you going to answer?" Khalil raises an eyebrow.

"Oh, right" I shake my head, answering the call, placing the phone to my ear "Is this a matter of life or death?"

I immediately ask my friend, who lets out a long sigh.

"When is my worst female version going to leave?" Logan grumbles, which makes me smile.

I sit on the bed, Khalil in front of me with his arms crossed.

"The taste of victory is so sweet" I tease him about his unhappiness.

"Elahe, you little cheating Arab, this woman is literally a ticking time bomb" my friend speaks in his exaggerated voice.

"Did something happen? Or rather, something more?"

"Maybe the fact that she brought a man to her apartment and made a point of banging the bed against the wall all night long is reason enough for me to be not only pissed off but wanting to send her back to Brazil."

Logan is my apartment neighbor, and we've always been good neighbors, and maybe Nanda is causing him a bit of trouble.

"Nothing I haven't been through before, remember the times I had to text you in the middle of the night?"

"OH MY GOD, I swear I'll personally shove her back to Brazil..." I can't help but laugh.

"Let's not be dramatic, Logan. Fernanda is your best version, are you losing to a woman? You're like a baby crying on the phone here. While she's enjoying the men of Santa Monica, you're here whining, getting screwed over — maybe I threw a bit more fuel on the fire.

"Logan Miller getting screwed over? Never..." and without even saying goodbye, he left me with the *tu tu tu* of the call ending.

That's so typical of Logan.

"I didn't know you and Fernanda were friends" Khalil raises an eyebrow.

"It depends on what you call friendship. We talk every day since she moved to Los Angeles. At first, I felt lonely, and I would message her asking how things were going, and soon she started sharing everything, even sending me videos of the customers at the bar. It helped me ease my homesickness. Can you believe she and Maggie became friends?"

"Maggie was Rafiq's nanny?" he asks, confused.

"Yes, but Logan moved her return to Santa Monica up..."

"Oh, I know, she sent me a five-minute audio with a lot of laughter" Khalil cuts me off "Are you sure these two together won't cause a small war over there? Fernanda isn't the type to stay quiet when provoked; she might take the lecture, but then she'll hit back in the same coin."

"I think I added some fuel to the fire, Logan will probably come with a heavy hand — I close my eyes, shaking my head — Should I warn Fernanda? What if he shows up at his apartment with several women just to get back at her?"

I bite my lip, worried about my new friendship.

"And what if you let them duke it out? No one warned me back in my turn, let them be alone..." Khalil shrugs.

Khalil has never shown jealousy over the friend who is dating several men; on the contrary, he seems to know what she's up to and even supports it.

He really doesn't feel anything for her anymore. And by Allah, I don't feel jealous seeing their relationship.

I think they've made it clear on several occasions that they no longer feel anything for each other, and Nanda has been my distraction these thirty days, showing her loyalty to me. I hear a noise at the door, Khalil turns, going toward it, opening it just a crack and grabbing a suitcase that was handed to him. I soon recognize it as my suitcase.

"Did you have them bring my suitcase?" I ask, raising an eyebrow.

"Yes, I did. Is there a problem?" Khalil drags the bag, placing it next to the bed.

"No problem..."

Khalil remains standing, in the same position as before, with his arms crossed, as if he wants to say something.

"What's killing you, why are you looking at me like that?" I ask.

"Have you been eating well, Elahe?"

"Oh, what a strange question" I frown at his inquiry.

"I'm asking because you seem lighter. I held you in my arms the last time you were here, and I noticed a significant difference in your weight."

"Maybe the difference is that you've been exercising too much?"

"I don't think that would confuse the weights" Khalil rolls his eyes "Answer me, Elahe, don't dodge the subject."

"Always so protective" I huff as I see him sit beside me.

"You're not expecting me to spank you now, are you?"

"It was instinctive" I give a forced smile "It's not that I haven't been eating well, but lately my stomach hasn't been great, and some smells have become sensitive to my nose. I wanted to talk to you about this, but well... I was ignored."

Khalil raises his hand, touching my chin.

"What do you want to talk about?"

"I want to talk about the possibility that I might be pregnant. My period hasn't come since I left Los Angeles, and every time we didn't use protection."

"Are you insinuating that I'm going to be a father?"

"Technically, you already are a father" I shrug.

"Yes, that's true, but it's different. I'll be able to see our child grow in your belly!" His eyes become bright.

"Yes, you'll be able to see our child grow right here" I hold his hand, guiding it to my belly.

"Me, you, our boy, and another baby" he repeats.

"Yes, the four of us. But first, I need to take a test, I'm not sure yet" I declare fearfully.

"Well, I'm almost certain our second child is on the way" right at that moment, my stomach chooses to make a noise "Are you hungry?"

"I think so. It's getting too strange. If I'm pregnant, I'll need a doctor. It wasn't like this with Rafiq..."

"Helena must know a female obstetrician" he emphasizes the word female.

That's so typical of him.

"Now let's get dressed, you need to eat. And I bet everyone is downstairs, waiting to see if we kill each other or make up."

"I wouldn't bet on it, because I'm almost sure they are doing just that."

CHAPTER THIRTY-SEVEN

Elahe

Khalil holds the tip of my finger as we descend the palace stairs, concealing the gesture, and then he lets it go.

"What are you going to say to them?" I murmur.

"Do you want to hear the truth?" He lowers his intense dark eyes toward me "I can't stand being away from you anymore, and now that all of this is possible, I want to announce to everyone that you will be my wife forever."

He didn't smile, make any gesture, just gazed at me with his determined eyes.

"Forever is a long time, isn't it?" A trembling smile appears on my lips.

"Forever won't be enough for everything I want to do with you" A small hint of a smile appears on his lips.

At that very moment, we enter the dining room, where many had already dined, but some places were still occupied, including by Fazza, Helena, and Lâmia.

"I thought I asked for your help, mother" Khalil quickly spoke, pulling out a chair for me to sit beside him.

"I judged by the lack of shouting that everything was fine" The woman shrugged.

"I'd bet my fortune that there was never a call" The son questioned his mother.

"How presumptuous of my son" Lâmia makes a scene trying to hide her smile.

"Are you feeling better, Elahe?" Helena directs her words to me.

As they handed me my plate, I adjusted myself in the chair, responding to her:

"Yes, I am. I think it was just a bout of discomfort. Maybe being nervous made me feel that way" I try to come up with an excuse.

"Sorry I didn't go with you. Well, my condition isn't the best. If I had gone, we might have both ended up sick" Helena lets a smile slip out.

"Oh, are you pregnant?" I ask the obvious.

"Yes, we're expecting another child..."

"Another one of many" Fazza murmurs proudly.

"That's because you're not the one carrying it for nine months and then dealing with a mini version of the father" Helena rolls her eyes.

"Have you considered..." Lâmia begins to speak, wiping her mouth with a napkin "Helena and Elahe pregnant at the same time?"

All eyes turn to me, as if expecting me to say something about it.

"I... I..." I start to speak, but nothing comes out.

"Elahe isn't sure if she's pregnant, it's just a suspicion. If she is pregnant, we'll resume our marriage" Khalil answers for me.

"Only if she's pregnant?" Fazza raises an eyebrow, confused.

"What more do you want?" Khalil holds my hand under the table as if signaling me to stay silent.

"Nothing, you must know what you're doing" Fazza's brother just shakes his head.

"I think you're both stubborn. It's so obvious that you feel something for each other, and yet you're being coy" Fazza gives his wife a stern look "Oh, come on! If no one says it, I will! Khalil is so smart about some things and proud about others, no one in this palace can stand his bad mood."

"I'll excuse you for being pregnant, sister-in-law. It must be the hormones talking" Khalil responds with a tone of mockery.

"Believe me, brother-in-law. It's not the hormones, it's the reality of the moment..." Helena emphasizes the word brother-in-law.

"Don't worry, your problems are solved, I hope they're the only ones" Khalil mocks his sister-in-law again.

"What are you talking about?" Fazza and Lâmia ask simultaneously.

Khalil looks in my direction, and we exchange glances for a few seconds. Knowing that this is what we both want, to be beside each other.

"We decided" Khalil begins to speak, pausing as he looks at his family in front of us "That we're resuming our marriage, that the divorce was a mistake, but a necessary one. Only distance made me realize how wrong I was, seeing you away made me miss you even more, and as the saying goes, only when you lose do you realize its value. I don't want to be away from Elahe anymore, and if she dares to disappear again, I'll tie her to the foot of the bed..."

He turns his face toward me, seeing my forced smile, which makes him laugh.

"Just kidding, no tying..." he winks, leaving room for second intentions.

"By Allah!" Fazza thanks, looking up "I thought this moment would never come. And if it's any consolation, you were never really separated..."

"How so?" Khalil cuts off his brother before he can finish.

"Well, technically, yes. But your contract hasn't been finalized yet. I have a copy, and Hassan has another. We were waiting for this first month to see if you would change your minds" Fazza clasps his hands on the table.

"Did you know about this, Elahe?" Khalil asks me.

I leave the utensils beside the table.

"No, like you, I'm surprised, but not shocked" I gently shrug my shoulder.

"Of course, you shouldn't be surprised by anything anymore" Khalil lets out a long sigh "Did you make me blind without reason?"

"Technically, we just let the two of you follow your path. If you had decided to proceed with the divorce, the paperwork would have gone through" his brother responds to him.

"Then I ask you to tear it up" Khalil declares with an authoritative voice.

"Is this really what you want? Hassan would like to know about this too..."

"Send my brother-in-law to the palace, and we'll sort it out together" Khalil declares determinedly.

"Elahe?" Fazza turns his gaze toward me.

"Yes, this is what I want. We've spent too much time apart, all because of our pride. Now, I don't want to waste any more time away from my husband" I say, looking from one to the other "The lie almost separated us, but our feelings were stronger and united us once again."

A sincere smile escapes my lips, knowing that even though I want my freedom, for my love for Khalil, I can do anything. What's the point of having my freedom if my thoughts are on the man I love? That's why I will always choose Khalil; he may be somewhat possessive, but he's willing to change, or at least that's what I hope.

I finish eating the first course of the meal when one of the servants appears to remove it. Distractedly, I lift my face, recognizing the gaze of the man, Ihab, the man who ruined me, that malevolent look that makes my entire body tremble. Instinctively, I grip my husband's hand tightly.

"Ihab..." I pronounce the name of that damned man.

CHAPTER THIRTY-EIGHT

Khalil

I turn my face, seeing the expression of distress in Elahe's eyes as she clutches my hand tightly.

When she utters that name.

"Ihab..."

What does she mean by that? Who is this man?

"Elahe, what's happening?" I ask, somewhat astonished.

"Please, get me out of here, Khalil" she pleads, her voice faltering "I can't stay in this palace, I can't..."

Her voice fades as she stands up abruptly. I do the same, pulling her close to me, while the man who removed the plate from the table watches the scene.

"What are you talking about?" I ask again, noticing that, like me, no one else understands what's going on.

"How dare you, Ihab, how dare you?" she calls him by name.

"You're mistaken, madam, that's not my name" the man finally speaks.

"I'm not crazy; I'd recognize him even if I were blind, you bastard!" I quickly place myself in front of her, intending to protect her from whatever is happening.

"Sorry, you must be mistaken, I don't know what you're talking about" Ihab shakes his head.

Fazza, who had been sitting, stands up.

"What's going on here?" My brother immediately assumes his role as the ruler of the palace.

"It must be a mistake, I'll leave" the man turns his back.

"Get me out of here, get our child out of here, he... he..." Elahe speaks again behind me, her hand gripping my shirt tightly.

"What are you talking about?" I ask, lowering my face to see her completely curled up behind me.

"It's him, Khalil, it's him..." I can see her closing her eyes in her distress, seeking support from me.

My mother joins us, holding Elahe's shoulder.

"Ihab, the man who ruined me" Elahe murmurs so quietly that I only understand by reading her trembling lips.

My hands clench into fists, as if a dark cloud has taken over my eyes, everything turning completely black, rage consuming my body.

I clench my fists, knowing that my mother is beside her, wanting to kill the man who dared to take advantage of an eighteen-year-old girl.

Ihab barely had time to take three steps before I was yanking him by the collar of his tunic, gripping him so hard that he was startled.

Turning towards me, he began to speak:

"I don't know what she's talking about, I don't know this woman..."

"Are you calling my wife crazy?" He didn't get a chance to say anything more as my clenched fist rose, landing a punch on his face, making him try to defend himself.

"She's crazy, I don't know her!" He continues to defend himself.

I find myself completely blinded by rage, unable to focus on anything they're saying around me. I raise my hand, delivering another punch to his nose, pushing him against the wall, and hitting him in the stomach with my elbow, hearing him groan in pain.

"No one, absolutely no one can call her crazy, you bastard! You'll regret the day you dared to lay a finger on her" I press my forearm against his neck "You filthy worm! You don't deserve to be called a man..."

I spit the words in his face, my face close to his, seeing the reflection of fear in his wide eyes. Elahe's words come to my mind, remembering how terrified she was, the fear she felt when she told me what happened, flooding my thoughts, making me even more blinded by rage.

"Let me go..." he pleads with a faltering voice.

"Now admit it's not you" I murmur as if I've found the worst part of myself.

"I'm... I'm... I..." he's almost closing his eyes when the strong hands of my two brothers pull me back, causing the bastard to fall to the ground.

I pull my body forward in a moment of their slip, kicking the bastard who took advantage of Elahe.

"Khalil, brother, you'll kill him! Do you want to carry someone's death on your shoulders?" Fazza says in my ear, loudly, to make me process this information.

"This bastard I'll carry on both my shoulders" I declare, wanting to escape from them.

"We'll send him to our rights..."

"I want him rotting in jail" I cut off my brother's words "I want him lynched in public."

The rage continues to blind me.

Until I feel that sweet touch on my face, making me lower my face. There she is, cheeks flushed, eyes wet with tears, long black lashes damp with the water falling from her eyes.

Damn, I scared her.

"Elahe..." I murmur her name like a lifeline.

"You are and always will be my greatest protector" she whispers with a broken voice "But don't kill him, that's not you..."

"He touched you" I declare incredulously.

"And you made me forget that horrible day, you make me believe there is another person who completes my happiness" Fazza and Omar are still by my side, holding onto my arm. It took both of them to pull me off the bastard who is still lying on the ground "I love you, Khalil, please don't do this, even though I know he deserves it, even though I want to do it with my own hands, I believe your brother has some way of tossing him into a back alley and making him suffer like I suffered..."

"No..." the man murmurs to the ground.

"I won't let him escape like Hassan did. We have no scandal to avoid; we've been involved in worse scandals. What's one more?" I declare, looking to both sides and asking my brothers "I won't do anything, you can let me go."

Reluctantly, they release me. Feeling dirty for having touched the bastard on the ground, I don't reach out to my wife, fighting against all the demons to go back to the man and finish what I started. I turn to Fazza, asking:

"Promise me you'll make him pay for everything he did to Elahe?"

"Yes, brother, I promise. Now go, don't stain your aura with someone who doesn't deserve your time."

I nod, lowering my face as I search for my wife, who gave a small signal for me to follow her.

Elahe is shaken, completely beside herself, needing all the comfort I can give her. My wife needs me, and I know Fazza will give the bastard who dared to exploit a woman's vulnerabilities the worst fate possible.

CHAPTER THIRTY-NINE

Elahe

Khalil interlaces his fingers with mine, guiding me up the stairs. We ascend in silence. The image of my husband still in my mind, him out of control, nearly killing Ihab. I won't lie; part of me wanted him to go through with it, to ruin Ihab as he ruined me.

He did it for me. Khalil wanted to make Ihab feel what I felt. It took Omar's help to get Fazza to pull Khalil off Ihab. Nothing made him let go, as if he were blind, completely deaf.

We enter his room, where he immediately pulls me into his arms, pressing me against his hard chest. I draw in a deep breath, feeling his scent overwhelm my senses.

"Sorry if I frightened you, that wasn't my intention" he murmurs, resting his chin on my head.

"You didn't frighten me" I whisper, lifting my head.

Our eyes meet.

"I wanted to kill that man. I've never felt such rage as I did today, knowing he touched you without your consent, something inside me took over, something I've never felt before" his hand lifts, holding my chin, tracing my lips.

"What scared me the most was knowing he was here, the man I thought was far from me..." my body trembles in fear.

"No one will ever dare to touch you again. Know that you are mine, and I'm capable of any madness to keep those sad eyes from me. Your happiness is my happiness. If someone hurts you, they are hurting me. When it comes to my family, I will protect them with all my strength."

I raise my hand, trailing it along his neck, feeling the tips of his hair.

Running his hand through my hair, he removes my hijab, letting it fall to the floor.

"I need a shower..." he murmurs "I can't stand the thought of possibly smelling like that bastard, but I need something else."

His face lowers, holding both sides of my cheeks.

"Thank you..." I murmur, his lips brushing mine "Today I saw the difference between the man who would do anything to protect me and the one who only wanted to ruin me. You may have all your flaws, but you're the whole package I love."

I clutch his shirt, feeling his heart race.

A small smile forms at the corner of his lips, our mouths meeting in a kiss, slow and tender, his tongue entering my mouth, seeking passage.

I return the kiss, sighing with his hold on my waist.

Moved by the moment, he picks me up, carrying me to the bed, laying me down, coming over me, his hand smoothing my cheek, moving our faces apart.

Words are unnecessary at that moment, as he begins to unbutton his shirt, standing and tossing the fabric to the floor, opening the first button of his pants. My eyes are fixed on his bare, hairless chest, revealing smooth skin.

He lowers his pants, leaving only his black boxer briefs, outlining his thigh.

He extends his hand to me, I hold onto his firm fingers, standing in front of him. Khalil turns me around, unbuttoning my tunic, letting it fall to the floor, pushing my hair to the side as he kisses my bare neck. Causing me to shiver all over, he unhooks my bra, the garment falling to the floor along with our other clothes.

I turn to face him.

"So beautiful" he murmurs, his face descending toward mine "Say that everything we did in the past will stay in the past, that we will start a new future together?"

"Yes..." my voice comes out weak, dying without completing the sentence.

"Promise me you'll be mine, every day of our lives?" His hand grips my hair, pulling it back with precision.

"I promise, my Sheikh, I will be yours, I am yours, only yours" I bite my lips at the pleasurable pain in my hair.

"Say it again?" He asks, pushing me onto the mattress, coming over me.

His body presses against mine, that necessary and yet suffocating contact.

"I am yours, my Sheikh. Nothing and no one will change my feelings for you. What's the point of freedom if it doesn't bring you to me?" he lifts his body, bringing our lips together in another kiss.

"This time apart was enough proof that our destiny is to be together..."

"Together" I repeat the word.

"I love you, my own, only mine" his face travels down my neck, leaving trails of kisses along the way.

Reaching the middle of my breasts, I throw my head back, a sigh escaping my mouth as he takes one of my breasts in his mouth, biting down hard on the nipple, then circling his tongue over the sensitive spot.

"I need to bury myself in your curves" he murmurs against my heated skin "I need to feel your pussy writhing on my cock..."

His words die as he presses his member, trapped in his underwear, against my body.

"Please, Khalil" I plead with a trembling voice.

In a swift motion, he removes his underwear, doing the same with mine, discarding our intimate garments.

Khalil has me sit on him, pressing his penis into my intimacy, which he helps to guide inside.

"Elahe... ah... my Elahe" he murmurs as I sit on his member.

I grip his chest, moving back and forth, with the impact of the movement, grinding on him. I scratch his skin, biting my lip hard.

My hair falls in long cascades around my head, his eyes locked on mine, his hands spread across my buttocks, aiding the movements.

"You are the definition of perfection" he murmurs, squeezing my buttocks tightly.

Before I have a chance to say anything, he puts me on all fours. The movement makes me gasp and let out a little squeal with the slap he gives my buttocks.

"Stick that little butt out for me..."

"Like this? Like this?" I don't let him finish the sentence, sticking my butt out, biting my lip in response to his smile.

"Yes, just like that" his hand smooths over my skin, delivering another slap "It's almost impossible to resist the itch I have in my hand, it's as if everything about you awakens my most possessive side, wanting to mark you as mine at all times."

In the midst of his words, he starts penetrating me again, this time more forcefully, going deep, his pelvis slamming into my buttocks. Our sweaty bodies, the echo of our intimate act becoming muffled within the room. It didn't take much to suppress a moan, letting that overwhelming sensation take over, surrendering to orgasm, with long spasms coursing through my body.

Khalil roars my name, thrusting strongly one last time, feeling that liquid fill me up, soon making us collapse exhausted on the bed.

We lie in silence, only our irregular breaths becoming present, until they calm down.

My husband pulls me against his sweaty chest, and I don't even care.

"Damn, how I missed this" he murmurs with his chin resting on my head "I swear if you think about staying away from me again, I'll lock you at the foot of the bed. Never dare to think you can live away from me again, Elahe. You need to understand that you are mine. And if you think you're not, I'll make you..."

I let out a weak laugh at what he said.

"That's so like you" I murmur amid a yawn "Today was a long day. I can say it was the most intense one..."

"Well, I have to agree with you on that" he murmurs "Let's take a shower. And then I want to get Rafiq to sleep with us tonight. I need to have in my mind my wife waking up with me and our son, and then ending the day well..."

I lift my face, finding a weary smile on his lips.

"I'll always blame myself for how I handled the divorce..."

"But it was necessary. I needed to feel the pain of losing you... losing you for real" he completes my thought.

I touch his beard, feeling his face in my hand, my fingers smoothing over every part of him.

"Let's take a shower. I'm eager to bring our boy to us tonight" with his help, I get up from the bed.

CHAPTER FORTY

Elahe

"Can I?" I hear my son's childish voice, making me smile in my sleep.

"Mommy is sleeping," Khalil whispers to the little one.

I squeeze my eyelids shut, listening to their interaction.

"Just a little, can I?" Rafiq has improved his speech, and it's so delightful to hear his tiny baby voice being pronounced.

Slowly, I open my eyes, finding pairs of eyes directed at me.

"Mommy" I'm startled to see my little one throw himself into my lap.

"What a nice hug!" I declare, feeling his sweet child scent.

"I think now you can," Khalil says.

Rafiq quickly stands up, trying to jump into our midst, which doesn't go well and causes him to fall several times, needing Khalil to lift him, who is amused by our son's commotion. He holds his hand, helping him get up, and uses his hand as support for our son to jump on the bed.

I sit on the bed, observing the father and son scene, both so alike, the same smile, the same sideways look as they smile.

I wonder how such resemblance is possible. At this moment, Khalil looks sideways, catching me in the act of observing them. Rafiq throws himself onto the bed, lying down between us.

"I hope nothing bad is going through that little head" he smiles, leaning in and giving a kiss on my forehead.

"Actually, there is something..."

"Sheikha Elahe, don't start with that, or I'll go right after a chain" he declares with a teasing smile on his face.

"No, no, no, it's not what you're thinking..."

"So what's on your mind?" he asks, raising an eyebrow in a lovely way.

"If you let me finish speaking, I can conclude my thought" I shake my head, watching Rafiq's little arms reach out to his father.

It's incredible, their relationship, as if they were destined to be father and son.

Khalil lowers his gaze, holding our son's hand. Rafiq throws himself against his chest, hugging his father's abdomen, with his face turned sideways, resting his head there. Khalil lifts his hand, gently stroking his son's hair.

"He is simply the best thing we could have done together" Khalil declares, kissing our son's head.

"From the beginning, you always treated him as a son, you never had doubts? After all, we had the DNA test done through your brother" I ask a bit hesitantly.

"Look at him and then at me. Unless I have a lost twin brother out there, he is my son, and it's not necessary to expose this little diamond to that. Knowing for sure it will be positive for my paternity. He was born to be mine, and I will make up for this first year lost by my side, for the rest of my life..." Khalil lets the sentence die, embracing our son, his affection revealing all the love he feels for the little one.

A smile escapes me, biting the tip of my lip, completely forgetting what I was going to say.

"What were you going to say?" he asks.

"Oh, right" I shake my head "I know you're used to living with your family, but living these two years away made me realize I could have more privacy in a quieter place, not so busy, with people not constantly intruding on our personal matters."

"What do you have in mind?" Khalil raises an eyebrow.

"On the day I went to the stud farm with Helena, I noticed that you have a house there too..."

I let the sentence die, waiting for some reaction from him.

"That house is old" Khalil makes a face "But the idea isn't bad. And if I ask them to renovate it, adding a bit of us there?"

"Are you saying I can help with the decoration?" I clap my hands somewhat excitedly.

"Of course! Let's ask Fazza for permission, since that mansion belongs to the family. But I'm sure he'll agree, all to keep me from moving to another country..."

I don't let him finish, throwing myself into the embrace of him and Rafiq, hearing our son's loud laughter.

KHALIL HELD RAFIQ IN his lap, hearing laughter coming from the living room and recognizing that childlike giggle—it's Latifa.

"Is Hassan here?" I frown, looking at my husband.

"He is. Fazza sent me a message to let me know; I just didn't tell you because I wanted to enjoy more time with my wife and son" he winks with his charming eye.

We enter the living room, and I quickly spot Hassan sitting on the sofa next to my sister-in-law Malika. Abdul and Ayda are also there, which makes me frown.

"Are all the Al-Bughdadi here?" I ask without even greeting them.

"Almost everyone" Zenda, my mother, whom I hadn't seen, is sitting next to Lâmia.

"Even you, Mom?" I roll my eyes.

"When I found out everything that happened, I had to come along."

My eyes meet Hassan's, making it clear by his raised eyebrow that he already knew everything.

"Pimo Fifiq" I lower my face, seeing the little girl with black hair and two intense green spheres.

Latifa was calling for Rafiq, who was in Khalil's lap. My son jumps to the floor, wanting to go with his cousin. He immediately grabs the girl's hand, going to the center of the room, where Hakan, Abdul's son, and Zayn and Mohammad, sons of Fazza and Helena, are.

Among the younger ones, Latifa is the only girl; Fazza's daughters aren't there.

Hassan stands up, his tall frame always looking with eagle eyes, heading towards my husband. Stopping in front of him, I turn my face, startled to notice that Hassan pulled him into a hug. My brother gave him a pat on the back, clearly showing all his respect for Khalil.

"Never thought I'd say this, but you did what I should have done years ago. Welcome to our family. It's good to know you two have finally reconciled" Hassan says amidst the hug.

"You shouldn't thank me, because I would have killed the bastard without a second thought, just as I'll do the same to anyone who dares to touch my wife."

Khalil declares loudly, the two of them part, looking into each other's eyes.

"Elahe" my brother looks in my direction "You know that everything I've always done was for your best, fulfilling all your wishes, no matter how crazy they were..."

"I always knew you knew where she was" Khalil cuts off my brother, snorting.

"Yes, my Sheikh, my entire family knew. Their loyalty to me was tested, and only I know how horrible it was for them. But that whole day..." I shook my head, trying to forget Khalil's words, denying them.

I feel my husband's hand on my back.

"Remind me never to act on impulse, since you have the habit of doing the same" Khalil lowers his head, letting a sideways smile escape.

"And now, since we're on the subject. About your marriage" Hassan declares, sitting back down next to my sister-in-law.

Once again, my personal life is being discussed in front of my whole family.

"I want to know too. After all, I found out yesterday that we're not divorced" Khalil crosses his arms, looking from his brother to me.

"Technically you are, but the last copy of the contract is here. We removed it from the document system, and there's only this original one that was with Fazza" Hassan takes the papers Abdul handed to him "The media reported that you were divorced, but as the head of my Emirate and Fazza as the head of his Emirate, we decided to hold on to the copies, and here they are. Elahe."

My brother calls my name, extending his hand towards me, making a gesture for me to take the papers from him. My eyes meet Mali's; she has a sincere smile on her lips, as if saying, *I always knew your destiny was to end up together.*

I hold the papers in my hands, deciding my future, to move forward and end the divorce with Khalil. My eyes find Rafiq sitting on the floor, a toothless smile on his face, his hair messy as he plays with his cousins. I lift my gaze, meeting Khalil's, the reason I fled, the reason I came back. I have no doubts about my decision.

It's him, it's always been him, my husband, my man, my Sheikh.

Since the first time I fell on that fence at my brother's stud farm, from his hands touching my body.

"What good is freedom if it doesn't bring you to me" I whisper with a trembling voice.

I hold the papers with both hands, tearing them up.

Khalil, who seemed to be holding his breath, exhales with difficulty.

"By Allah, if you had said you accepted this divorce, I would have thrown myself at your feet and never let go" he mocks amidst his desperation, causing laughter from Fazza, Hassan, and Abdul to fill the room.

"There's not a man alive who wouldn't fall to his knees for a woman" Abdul jokes "We completely understand you, brother-in-law."

Breaking protocol, Khalil pulls me into his arms, hugging me tightly against his chest.

"I will be eternally yours, only yours, my Elahe..." he murmurs amidst the embrace.

"I love you, my *possessive Sheikh*..." I whisper with a smile on my lips.

CHAPTER FORTY-ONE

Khalil

ONE MONTH LATER...

Will it take long to start growing? I scratch my beard, tilting my head as I watch Elahe walk hand in hand with Rafiq.

She's always been strong, not caring about what people say about her. Even though we were once again targets of sensationalist websites, Elahe never showed any signs of being disheartened. Our return was announced, and everyone thought we were going to marry again, until the Agu Dhami palace issued a statement clarifying that a second marriage would not happen, not while the first was still valid. Knowing that in the end, she chose to stay by my side made me a tremendously lucky man.

Elahe chose me, despite giving her plenty of reasons to walk away, she chose me.

Damn! If this isn't love, I don't know what the hell love is.

It's only been two days since we moved to the mansion next to the stud farm; I never imagined Elahe would be so radiant living in this place.

"Daddyyyy" Rafiq notices my presence, letting go of his mother's hand and coming towards me.

I descend the two steps from the veranda.

I open my arms to take him into my lap.

"I see someone took mommy out early to the stable, or was it the other way around?" I ask, seeing Elahe approaching us.

"You were on a video conference with the Americans, so I decided to take Rafiq for a walk" she shrugs.

"Horse" Rafiq repeats what they went to see, imitating the horse's whinny, making me laugh along with his mother.

"I think I'm going to be at a disadvantage here" I joke, knowing Elahe's love for animals, and Rafiq is following in the same direction.

"Hassan said Hadi is already at his stud farm, and he's going to send him here" Elahe declares excitedly.

Hadi is her horse, which she's been away from for a long time.

"Are you sure?" I ask, concerned "I'm not against him being here, I just don't like the idea of seeing you riding a horse. Remember what the doctor said."

I begin voicing my worries.

"Don't worry, my Sheikh, I won't be riding Hadi..."

"Not riding him, or any other animal, until our son is here, safe and sound" I try to lighten the mood, making a joke.

"And we have the first sign of possessiveness of the day" Elahe rolls her eyes, shaking her head.

She has the habit of counting how many times I treat her with protection. My fear of losing her and the fear of something happening to our unborn child makes me somewhat possessive.

"Just precaution" I wink, extending my hand to her, which she holds at the tip of my finger while I carry our son in my lap.

Living in this mansion was the best thing we did; it doesn't have the same number of people as the palace, the staff is discreet, and in return, I can share affection with my wife.

"Nanda called me" Elahe says, letting out a long sigh.

"Problems?" I turn my face, seeing her distant expression.

"It seems she and Logan decided to end things. She's leaving California and going back to Brazil" Elahe shakes her head.

"We'll never know what made them break up..."

"Yes, we will. She said Logan is a *badboy* who is extremely immature, irresponsible, and doesn't honor his commitments" Elahe frowns in a funny way "And it didn't stop there; she called him a few more ugly names. I think it's all because Logan doesn't want to accept that he needs to come back and face his responsibilities. In other words, two stubborn heads. He who always made it clear that he would never speak to his paternal family again, and she who values good family relationships."

I shake my head, leaving my shoes by the door, my bare feet dragging on the floor.

"And did Logan call you?" I ask, wanting to hear his side.

"Of course he did" Elahe huffs, which makes me squint my eyes at her "Calm down..."

"You know how much I hate it when you huff around me..." we change the subject, quickly returning to talk about the couple.

"Has anyone ever told you that your quirks are pretty strange?" My wife joins me, and before I can respond, she continues "Back to the main topic, Logan is pretending to be *'I don't care what she thinks'*, which we know is a big lie. My friend has never stayed with someone for more than a week, and with Fernanda, it was different; they had been together for almost a month. Logan doesn't want to admit that Nanda is right."

"He needs to understand that most of the time, women are right" I shake my head, seeing a victorious smile on her lips "Did I mention that it's most of the time, right? Because there's that 1%..."

Elahe shakes her head, letting out a forced laugh.

Soon, we change the subject and enter the living room, where Rafiq asked to be put on the floor.

"Do I need to mentally prepare myself in case our child turns out to be a girl?" I turn my face, seeing a triumphant smile on my wife's lips.

"I won't lie, I'm hoping for a girl, so I don't end up at a disadvantage."

"Do you want to see me go gray before my time?"

"Which I highly doubt will happen, not with this abundance of black hair" Elahe jokes as she heads to the sofa and sits down.

Her eyes are fixed on our son, standing and leaning on the coffee table, playing with the decorations. Since nothing seemed dangerous, we let him explore his curiosity. I find myself analyzing my wife's features.

Of all the mistakes I've made in this life, Elahe has been my greatest success.

I am completely in love with this woman.

Waking up every day next to her is what I want to do for the rest of my life. It might sound like a huge cliché, but she is the air I breathe, the one my heart needs.

Without a doubt, being away from her for two years was worth it to have her by my side. Maybe I've always loved her, maybe from the moment she fell into my lap it was love. It just took time to become real, to realize we wanted all of this.

A lie kept us apart, destiny brought us together. I might be extremely possessive, but it's all in wanting to protect the wife I have by my side.

She turned her face, her eyes meeting mine.

"Any problem, my Sheikh?" she asks, raising an eyebrow.

"Is it going to be a long wait until we have our child?" I ask with a hint of sarcasm.

"Depends on what you consider, about eight to seven months" she lets that same smile I love escape from her rosy lips.

"My hands itch every time I see you" I whisper.

"Sadistic" she murmurs "We shouldn't even be having relations."

"Good thing we don't take it literally. I refuse to spend nine months away from my wife" I imply what I really want to say between the lines.

Elahe shakes her head, her eyes lowering, making her beautiful black lashes brush against the bottom ones as she blinks slowly.

I think I am literally fascinated by my wife.

"Well, we're not the only ones. Helena, Malika, and Ayda said their husbands don't adhere to the nine months of celibacy" my wife shakes her head.

I walk over to her, sitting next to her, making her look in my direction, holding her chin.

"Understand, I will never let you leave my side again. My nights will all be spent with you, nothing and no one will be able to take you away from me. Our destiny was written, and we are made for each other. My sweet wife, I will love and protect you always, until my last breath" I murmur, seeing a beautiful smile appear on her lips.

"I love you so much..." her sentence dies out when Rafiq throws a decoration on the floor.

I quickly glance at him, going over and sitting beside him.

Elahe mostly dismisses the nanny, so we can enjoy our son in our privacy, in the bubble we've built in this mansion for the three of us, soon to be four.

I never thought I'd say this. But it's by the side of the woman who lied to me that I found happiness. How I love Elahe and everything she gives me, providing me with the best gifts a man can have — my children.

EPILOGUE

Elahe

I clench my hands, anxious. Listening to the audience applaud. This is Jade's first competition, and she's not even nervous.

"Relax, my love, look at our little girl" I hear my husband's voice beside me, whispering close to my ear.

A smile escapes my lips as I watch Jade gallop with her horse, the same one she's been training with since she was a little girl. Khalil calls her his little girl, even though we know that at 13, she's not so little anymore.

The scarf tightly wrapped around her head, covering all her hair, she clears the obstacles effortlessly, as if she was born to do this.

I grimace as I hear Rafiq whistling next to me, cupping his hands to his mouth, making that annoying sound.

"Rafiq, for *Allah*! Isn't it enough that I'm nervous, must you be so exaggerated?" I scold him as he bursts into laughter.

"Mom, relax, Jade *is* handling this just fine" He puts his hands in his pockets.

Rafiq came to spend the weekend with us to attend his sister's first competition since he lives in the United States, studying at Harvard, the same place where his father went.

At eighteen, he's following in his father's footsteps, though I tried to change him, it was impossible. It seems the genes won out, and before I knew it, my son was doing the same things as his father.

Except for one thing: I don't intend to place him in an arranged marriage. He will have the freedom to choose whoever he wants by his side, whether she is Arab or foreign, I don't want him to go through what Khalil and I went through.

My youngest daughter is performing impeccably.

It's hard to believe that this little whirlwind came from me. It seemed like just yesterday she took her first steps, and now she's on a horse, riding with mastery. I lower my face, watching my husband discreetly hold the tip of my finger.

Khalil always showing his discreet affections in public.

"GO JADE!" Kaleb shouted, leaning over the safety rail.

"Boy, don't climb there, it might fall!" I scolded my middle son "And don't tell me to relax!"

I declared, anticipating that, like his father and brother, he would tell me to relax.

"As always, the lecture falls on who?" Kaleb rolls his eyes, making Khalil and Rafiq's laughter come to the fore.

Kaleb, our middle child, always plays the victim, a characteristic of his, which makes him the center of attention in our home.

He recently turned sixteen and asked for nothing less than a lion like his uncle Fazza's and his children who love wild animals. Obviously, Khalil did not give him one. Fazza has these animals, but they are all trained and kept in a reserved area of the palace.

Kaleb came with an adventurous spirit that I struggle to understand where he got it from.

"Latifa is calling" Rafiq steps away to answer.

"Something tells me Rafiq knows something" I murmur, looking at my husband.

"I don't doubt that, but as we know, he won't say much, let alone about her. Those two keep many secrets from us" my husband shrugs as if it's normal.

"I hope she's not up to anything. After all, it was already a sacrifice for Hassan to let her study in America."

"Well, she's already a grown woman, isn't she?" Khalil tried to act nonchalant.

"Will you think the same when Jade is over eighteen?" I raised an eyebrow, seeing the grimace he made.

"Jade is different..."

"Tell that to my brother then" I tease, making him realize that the situation with them is the same.

Two protective fathers who guard their daughters from everything, even future boyfriends. Khalil can't even stand hearing the words Jade and boyfriend in the same sentence.

I find myself imagining how possessive this man will be when she becomes a grown woman.

"DAD, DID YOU SEE HOW I was the best?" Jade hugs her father around the waist, holding her medal in the other hand.

"My little girl, you were born to be the best" Khalil strokes our daughter's huge ego.

Our driver waits for us in the parking lot, while Kaleb and Rafiq are already in another car; those two stick together whenever Rafiq is home.

We get into the car, Jade between us as the driver starts the engine.

We spend the entire time listening to what our daughter has to say about her first competition, leaving us ecstatic with everything she has to share.

"WILL I GET A DANCE from my wife today?" I hear my husband's voice whispering in my ear as he embraces me from behind.

"It depends, I'm not sure if you deserve it" I tease, biting my lip.

Khalil loves to see me dance for him. So much so that I bought several *sexy* outfits just for us to use when we are alone, in the privacy of our bedroom.

At first, I was mortified, until I realized that by doing this, I get my husband exactly the way I want him, fulfilling all my desires.

Who am I kidding? Khalil is a lively man, loves to be wild behind closed doors, enjoys being dominant, but when I take control, he goes silent, rolling his eyes, begging for more of my touches.

"You know we need to replenish our stock, thanks to you who loves to tear my outfits" I declare, feeling his hand sliding up my nightgown.

"What can I do? I can't help it that you drive me crazy every time you have me under your spell, as if I were enchanted by every curve of your body, going wild seeing the wonderful wife I have in my arms..." I turn my body, lifting my head.

"Do you think this will ever end?" I ask, knowing that our marriage isn't always a bed of roses, but in bed, we always fit together perfectly.

"I could never get tired of you. Every day I wake up next to you, I'm sure I made the right choice, even though it wasn't always so at the beginning" a smile appears on his lips, knowing that running away from him was the craziest thing I ever did.

"I guess in the end..."

"It was always meant to be us" he completes my sentence "my wife, the mother of my children..."

"Speaking of children, did you see Kaleb come in when he came to the room?"

"Yes, he was coming from the stable" I nod.

Kaleb always checks on the horses before bed.

When Hadi, my horse, passed away, he was one of the ones who missed him the most. My son is very attached to the little details.

"Now back to the main topic..."

"Our main topics are always interrupted by a reminder of some child" I joke about the situation.

"I think they were the best things we ever did" my husband lowers his face, pressing his soft lips to mine.

Khalil may have his flaws, he is still extremely possessive with me and our children, but he's my Khalil, my Sheikh, the man my heart chose to love.

And I love him, I love him unconditionally.

THE END.

Did you love *The Sheikh's Forbidden Bride*? Then you should read *The Sheikh's Hidden Heart* by Amara Holt!

The Sheikh's Hidden Heart is a passionate, heart-stopping romance set in the enchanting world of the **Seven United Emirates**. Sheikh **Abdul Amin** has always guarded a **dark secret**, one that forces him to vow never to marry or fall in love. Love, to him, is a weakness he cannot afford. But when his brother, the powerful **emir**, arranges a marriage to the beautiful and **headstrong Ayda**, everything changes.

Ayda has been raised to fulfill her duty, but she never expected her union to be with a man as **mysterious** and distant as Abdul. Their marriage of **convenience** quickly turns into a battle of **wills** and desires as they are forced to navigate their complex feelings for each other.

But Abdul's **hidden heart** remains locked away. As **passion ignites** between them, the secret he has been guarding threatens to tear them apart. Can Ayda break down the walls around Abdul's heart, or will his past destroy any chance of love?

The Sheikh's Hidden Heart is perfect for fans of intense, **slow-burn romances** filled with secrets, power struggles, and undeniable **chemistry**. Will the Sheikh protect his wife and his heart, or will the **truth** push them further apart? Discover the love story that defies all odds.

About the Author

Amara Holt is a storyteller whose novels immerse readers in a whirlwind of suspense, action, romance and adventure. With a keen eye for detail and a talent for crafting intricate plots, Amara captivates her audience with every twist and turn. Her compelling characters and atmospheric settings transport readers to thrilling worlds where danger lurks around every corner.